DANCE WITH DEATH

I jerked upright, ears strained, every muscle tense. Suddenly I could no longer see the moon shining through the skylight. It had been blotted out by a large black shape.

And now the sound came again, that stealthy scraping and slithering across the roof – except that this time it was followed by a soft thud from somewhere directly outside.

I turned my head sharply towards the balcony. A scream rose to my lips and was stifled only because my throat was too tense to let it out. A dark shadow was lurking outside the double doors – the doors which I in my carelessness had left open.

I couldn't swear to it afterwards, but at the time I was almost certain it was the shadow of a man.

POINT CRIME

DANCE WITH DEATH

Jean Ure

SCHOLASTIC

Scholastic Children's Books
7–9 Pratt Street, London NW1 0AE, UK
a division of Scholastic Ltd
London ~ New York ~ Toronto ~ Sydney ~ Auckland

First published by Scholastic Ltd, 1995

Copyright © Jean Ure, 1995

ISBN 0 590 13319 5

All rights reserved

Typeset by TW Typesetting, Midsomer Norton, Avon

Printed by Cox & Wyman Ltd, Reading, Berks.

10 9 8 7 6 5 4 3 2 1

1

BUTCHER STRIKES AGAIN!
Being in a French tabloid the words were, as
you might expect, in French; and my French, as you
might also expect from someone who never took the
trouble to pay attention in school, is pretty basic.
Fine for ballet terms – *fondu, battement, croisés en
arrière* and all the rest; otherwise strictly *plume de
ma tante* stuff. Even I, however, was capable of
translating that screaming banner headline in
France Soir.

Another body found in Bois de Boulogne.

My blood did exactly what blood is always said to
do in these situations: it ran cold in my veins. Or at
any rate I broke out into goose pimples and my
hands went all clammy.

Claire! I thought. Could it be Claire?

Claire is my identical twin. *Absolutely* identical except that she has a purple birthmark in a rather personal place which I fortunately (as a dancer) managed to escape. Even though we're mirror images, we've never been as close as identical twins are supposed to be. "You're meant to love each other!" Mum would periodically wail during our childhood, as I tried to gouge out Claire's eyeballs with my fingernails and Claire did her best to push my teeth down my throat. For all that, I wouldn't like to think of my other half being brutally done to death and left to rot in a French ditch.

Where had it all sprung from, this nightmare? Why should I even begin to imagine that a body found in the Bois de Boulogne might belong to my twin?

It had all started off so well! I had been so excited, so looking forward to it, this trip to Paris with the Company. There I was, seventeen years old, only a humble member of the corps, to be sure – but what a corps! What a company! The Barbican was one of Britain's most distinguished dance groups. It was also the one in which my beloved Jean-Guy was premier danseur, and just to make matters totally and utterly blissful Jean-Guy had promised Mum that he would keep an eye on me on my first foreign tour. Of course I'd protested that it wasn't necessary – "I'll be all right! I'm going to stay with Claire!" – but I'd only done it half-heartedly.

I had worshipped the ground that Jean-Guy trod on for as long as I could remember. (Claire on the other hand has always been immune: Claire is so *sensible*. And anyway, Claire has never wanted to be a dancer.) Jean-Guy is five years older than we are and the son of Mum's dearest and oldest friend, from the days when they used to kick up their legs together doing the can-can in a Paris nightspot. When Jean-Guy said firmly that instead of staying with the rest of the principals in a swish hotel near the Champs-Elysées he would book into somewhere near Claire's flat in Neuilly, Mum said gratefully that that would put her mind at rest: "Vicky isn't like Claire. She's such a scatterbrain." Who was I to argue?

I remember sitting on the plane on the way to Charles de Gaulle (Jean-Guy was already over there). I remember watching some of the boys playing poker, and Marcia Stanforth hanging on the back of a seat watching them. I remember hugging myself and thinking here am I, Victoria Masters, member of a famous ballet company, on a plane, going to Paris, away from home...

Who knew what excitement might await me?

In the seat next to mine, Carmen Janigro was flicking through a book of ballet photographs. She came to a double-page spread of Jean-Guy – Jean-Guy in all his various personas, from noble and romantic in *Sylphides* to wild and exotic in *Corsair* –

and there for a moment she lingered. I lingered with her. Did a little sigh escape us?

"He isn't any use to you, you know."

"Pardon?" I jumped round. It was Marcia, another member of the Company. Senior to me, but not by all that much.

"I said –" she nodded towards Jean-Guy – "he isn't any use to you. No point getting your hopes up … wouldn't look twice in your direction."

"Well, no! I should think not!" I tried desperately to sound amused and indignant, rather than merely wistful. "A leading dancer looking at a lowly member of the corps?"

Marcia smiled. "They do, you'd be surprised … if they're that way inclined. But I'm afraid Jean-Guy simply isn't, ducky."

"Oh!" I gave a little laugh, light and airy. "I'm aware of *that*," I said, though in fact it had never so much as crossed my mind and came as something of a shock. Loads of men in ballet *are* the other way, of course; everyone just accepts it. But Jean-Guy? Jean-Guy, whom I'd sighed over and yearned after since I was knee high to a gatepost?

"Frightful waste, isn't it?" sighed Carmen.

She could say that again. I wondered if Auntie Vi (she's not our auntie but we always call her that, and Vi is short for Violetta, not Violet: she is part Russian, part English) I wondered if Auntie Vi knew that her one and only cherished offspring was the other way. Perhaps she wouldn't mind; she is very broad-minded. That is probably because she married a Frenchman who was a trapeze artist, and toured the world with him until one day the Frenchman ran off with a lady trapeze artist, whereupon Auntie Vi promptly forsook what she calls the biz, meaning show business, and settled down to run a little *pension* in the south of France.

Mum, in comparison, has led quite a sheltered existence. She gave up can-can dancing very early on to marry an accountant and have me and Claire, and has lived in Cricklewood ever since. You don't get much of "that sort of thing" in Cricklewood; not that I ever noticed. Mum would be really upset about Jean-Guy.

Not half as upset as I was! I suppose Jean-Guy could be described as every young girl's dream. (Unless you're a sensible young girl, like Claire.) He's not exactly the Incredible Hunk, though he is quite well built – the men have to be, in ballet, for hefting all those great lumping ballerinas about – but as one of our leading ballet critics once wrote, he is "beautifully put together". He is a knock-out when you see him on stage as Prince Siegfried or Albrecht. Some men don't have the figure for tights: Jean-Guy does. But he's just as much a knock-out when he's off stage, wearing grungy old jeans and a sweatshirt. He has this glorious glossy black hair (mine is depressingly curly and red), and what is more, he has *bone structure*.

Everyone in ballet longs for bone structure. Useless to have a face like a pudding, the spotlights will simply make it rounder and plumper and more puddingy than ever. Claire and I used to have faces like plum duffs when we were young, but thank heavens it was only puppy fat. We're now heart-shaped, with these rather big blue eyes and pointy chins. Jean-Guy's chin is definitely square – the sort of square that looks as if it's inviting upper cuts, or whatever it's called when someone slams a clenched fist at you.

What a waste! What a terrible waste! But I was glad all the same that Marcia had warned me. I don't believe in sighing over the unattainable. There, in the plane, I made a vow that from here on in I would look upon Jean-Guy as the brother I never had. It was glaringly obvious, now that I stopped to think about it, that he had long regarded me as a little sister. The other could never have been anything but a pipedream, anyway; I should have realized that when I saw him with the rest of the Company. Not that he was grand or stood on ceremony, but for all that Jean-Guy Fontenille was a leading dancer while Victoria Masters was a mere nothing, just one more swan in the back row of the corps; a big-eyed, pointy-chinned swan whom he had known since she was a drooling cygnet in nappies. Forget it, kid! Wise up and take off the rose-coloured spectacles. You're out in the big wide world now.

Yes, and the big wide world was beckoning me! I was actually looking forward to seeing Claire again. She had gone over to Paris eight months ago, on our seventeenth birthday, to be a full-time language student and live in a one-room apartment that belonged to an accountant friend of Dad's and was therefore known to be respectable. Mum hadn't minded Claire going to live on her own. She hadn't fussed and fretted as she did over me, because Claire was the sensible one, the practical one, the one who would always remember to eat proper meals and change the sheets on the bed and not stay out late with strange unsuitable men.

It had been Claire's idea that I should stay in the flat with her. "It will be fun," she had written, "being on our own. We'll have to share the same bed, but don't worry, it's quite large!"

We'd shared a bed once before, on a seaside holiday with Mum and Dad: we'd spent entire nights kicking at each other. But we'd been young, then. We were more tolerant now, more able to appreciate each other's good points and put up with the not-so-good. Claire might be a bit strait-laced and prosaic, but she was loyal, trustworthy, dependable. I felt a sudden overwhelming fondness for my twin as we disembarked at Charles de Gaulle. She was all right, was Claire!

The plan was that Jean-Guy would meet me off the airport bus (he was already in Paris for a TV show) and we would make our way to the flat together.

"Nice for some," said Marcia, as we boarded the bus.

"What's her problem?" Suzie Sheridan plonked herself next to me. Suzie and I had joined the Company together, six months ago. Neither of us had yet acquired Marcia's know-it-all cynicism.

"I think," I muttered, "she considers it a bit over-privileged for a member of the corps to be on speaking terms with one of the leading dancers."

"Well, of *course* it is," said Suzie. "Especially Jean-Guy ... but it's hardly your fault," she added, generously.

"She seems to think I'm pushing myself forward."

"Well, you're not. That's ridiculous. He doesn't normally take any more notice of you than he does of the rest of us."

That was true; no one had been more surprised than I when Jean-Guy had volunteered to keep an eye on me. I had to assume that Mum had spoken to Auntie Vi and that Auntie Vi had had one of her "little words" with Jean-Guy.

"Mind you," said Suzie – she knew all about the eye business – "you're lucky you've got a knight in shining armour. I reckon we could all do with one of those. Have you seen the headlines?"

"No," I said. "What headlines?" To be honest, I don't very often bother to look at newspapers.

"There's some maniac on the loose."

"What? In Paris?"

Suzie nodded. "They've already found three bodies."

"Ugh! Horrible." I shuddered. "I hope my mum doesn't get to hear of it. She's already having kittens … she thinks the entire male population of France is prowling the streets waiting to do dire and dreadful things to innocent British girls."

"This one actually is doing dire and dreadful things. They're calling him the Butcher of the Bois."

I ferreted about amongst the remnants of my schoolgirl French. Bois … wood?

"Bois de Boulogne," said Suzie. "It's where they've uncovered the bodies. It's really creepy."

I thought about it. It certainly wasn't very nice, but I couldn't get too worried over it. There was a remoteness about it, a sense of *nothing to do with us*.

"I'm just glad I'm staying in the hotel with all the others," said Suzie. "I don't think I'd be brave enough to do what you're doing."

"I think a hotel would be worse," I said. I wasn't going to let myself be panicked. "After all, you never know who's going to have a duplicate key to your room."

"Oh, gee, Vicky, thanks!" Suzie screeched in a high-pitched American accent. "Thanks a million! You've really made me feel great!"

Marcia, sitting in the seat ahead, twisted round to look at us.

"What's that in aid of?"

"She has just told me," moaned Suzie, "that the Butcher of the Bois is going to have a duplicate key to my hotel room!"

"I wish you wouldn't joke about it." That was Carmen, sitting next to Marcia. "It's not what I should call funny."

"Oh, now, come on!" Marcia spoke impatiently. "Surely you're not going to let one sick guy ruin the tour for you?"

"I'm certainly not going out after dark by myself, I can tell you that."

"Me neither," said Suzie. "For your information, the Bois de Boulogne is not a million miles from our hotel."

It was not a million miles from Claire's apartment in Neuilly, either, but fortunately I didn't know that then – though I daresay it wouldn't have bothered me even if I had. I was too busy savouring the thrill of being abroad, being with the Company – being with Jean-Guy, even if he wasn't ever going to look twice at me. I may have made a resolution to think of him as a brother, but these things take time. I had been in love with Jean-Guy for the better part of seventeen years; it wasn't a habit I could break just like that.

He was waiting for me, as promised, at the terminal. He didn't kiss me, not even in brotherly fashion, but then I wouldn't have expected him to. The rest of the Company were there: it would have looked very naff. Even as it was, I knew there were going to be buzzings and mutterings the minute our backs were turned. It hadn't taken me long to discover that ballet companies are hives of jealousy and petty (and not so petty) rivalries. I guess it comes of being so enclosed and of necessity cut off from the outside world.

"How was the trip?" said Jean-Guy.

I said that the trip had been great. I must have sounded childishly over-enthusiastic because Jean-Guy laughed and told me that when I had flown back and forth across the Channel as many times as he had just recently it would cease to be great and become nothing but one big bore.

"Oh, you're just blasé," I told him; and he raised his eyebrows and said, "Get her! Speaking French already!"

"When in Rome," I said.

"So, come on! Let's hear some!"

"*On dit*," I said carefully, just to show him that I could, "*que – il y a – un maniaque? Ici, à Paris?*"

His face darkened. "Some nutter; yes. I don't want you walking round by yourself. Wait for me

11

after the show every night and I'll see you back to the flat. Talking of which, had we better give Claire a quick ring and check she's there?"

"She'll be there," I said. She had written in her letter that she would wait in for us, and Claire always did what she said.

"*Quand même*, I think we'd better just ring," said Jean-Guy.

Needless to say I didn't have her telephone number, but fortunately Jean-Guy knew it. He always called Claire when he was over in Paris, just so he could report back to Mum that she wasn't in debt, on drugs, or pregnant. Not that anyone ever expected Claire to be any of those things, but Mum is anxious by nature.

Jean-Guy dialled the number and handed the receiver to me.

"Here you are. You talk to her."

"Hallo?" I said; but the phone was still ringing.

It went on ringing. And ringing.

The flat was obviously empty.

Jean-Guy shrugged. "Must have gone out."

"But she told me she'd be there!"

"So she forgot."

"Claire doesn't forget!"

"She's only human," said Jean-Guy. It was one of our jokes: was Claire human? The answer seemed to be yes. It still surprised me.

"Let's go and have a coffee, then try again."

"What's the time?" I said, as I followed Jean-Guy across the road.

"Just gone one. It's OK, we're not due at the theatre till two-thirty."

We had a full run-through on stage, then were free for that first evening, but I hadn't actually been thinking of the run-through. I'd been thinking of Claire.

"I *know* she wouldn't have forgotten, she was looking forward to it."

"So she popped out for something and got held up."

I shook my head. "She wouldn't have gone out if there was any chance of not getting back on time. You know what Claire's like." My twin sister is one of those people who work out how long it will take to get anywhere and then double it, just to be on the safe side.

"We'll give her another go in a few minutes," said Jean-Guy.

We drank our coffee, sitting on the pavement in the sunshine, then went back to try again. There was still no answer.

"We'd better get a cab," said Jean-Guy, "and go round there. Hopefully she'll be back by the time we arrive."

"It's very odd," I said. "It's not a bit like Claire."

It didn't occur to me to be worried; not seriously. Not at that stage. The worrying came later.

2

I said again, in the cab: "It really isn't like her."
I was the one who turned up late and forgot to
keep appointments, not my twin. Claire was the
most maddeningly reliable and responsible person
that I knew. (I say maddening because we were
always being compared – to my detriment. "Why
can't you be more like your twin?" our mum used to
wail when feckless Victoria, all haphazard and slap-
dash, loused something up for the umpteenth time.)

"Claire never lets people down!"

"So maybe she's changed. *Paree* –" Jean-Guy put
on his most exaggerated French accent, rolling his
r's ferociously in the back of his throat – "she does
strange sings to pipple."

"Not to Claire," I said. I'd been surprised Claire

had opted for Paris in the first place. Somewhere more sober would have seemed better suited to her. Brussels, say, or Lucerne.

"You'd be surprised," said Jean-Guy, reverting to his normal voice. "Betcha she's met up with some guy and got stars in her eyes and forgotten all about you."

I shook my head. "Not Claire," I said.

We reached rue Fleury, near the métro station Pont de Neuilly – a "good *quartier*" according to Jean-Guy – and the cab came to a halt outside Claire's apartment building. It was a small block, built of grey stone and quite old. There were only six other tenants beside Claire, plus the inevitable concierge. (I knew all about Claire's concierge, Mme Dastugue, for Claire had written to Mum about her. Mme Dastugue ruled the block with a rod of iron and could never be persuaded to do the simplest thing, not even take a message or receive a parcel, without a substantial *pourboire*, or tip.)

Claire lived on the top floor, in a sort of attic isolated from the rest. I pressed my finger on her bell, waiting for the intercom to crackle into life and for Claire's voice to say "Hallo?" and then, "Vicky! Did you try ringing me? I'm terribly sorry, I went out and forgot the time!" though really and truly, even now, I couldn't believe that Claire *would* forget.

"Try again," said Jean-Guy, so I did, with exactly the same result.

"She's obviously not here."

"No – out snogging with some man is my bet."

"At this time of day?"

"What's the matter with this time of day? There aren't any rules about it, are there?"

There probably would be, I thought, with Claire. But anyway, Claire wouldn't snog. I said so, forcibly, but Jean-Guy only laughed.

"Come off it! Seventeen, living in Paris, and not snogging?"

Not Claire, I thought.

"Did you," I said, "when you were seventeen?"

"You'd better believe it!"

I did believe it; all too easily. Jean-Guy is a very physical person. Claire, on the other hand, is quite contained and undemonstrative. Not only that, she has never been prey to the same all-consuming passions as the rest of us. I've quite lost count of the number of men I've been desperately in love with during the course of my life. (The only one to whom I had ever remained constant was Jean-Guy. Wouldn't you know it?)

"I'll just give the concierge a go, see if she's left any message." Jean-Guy stabbed his finger on the concierge's bell. "If not, we'd better go dump our bags at my place and come back later."

The concierge took her time in answering. While we were waiting it was on the tip of my tongue to be cheeky and ask Jean-Guy who he had done all his snogging with – except that why should he tell me the truth and what business was it of mine anyway? – but the concierge came shuffling out of her den before I could be tempted, which was probably just as well.

She looked us up and down in decidedly non-friendly fashion – the way you might look at a couple of typhus germs – and finally, grudgingly, made a grunting sound which may or may not have been a word of meaning in the French tongue. Jean-Guy explained (I think) that I was Mlle Victoria Masters *et la soeur de Claire Masters*, or he might have said *la jumelle*, which I happen to know is French for twin, though in fact he spoke far too fast for me to catch more than the odd word. When he'd finished, old Mme Dastugue mouthed something incomprehensible and waddled back into her cubby-hole.

"What did she say?" I said.

"She said she's got something for you."

It was just as well Jean-Guy was there for I would have been lost without him.

Mme Dastugue came shambling back. (She was like every concierge you've ever read about: old, shapeless, and totally disobliging.)

"*Voilà.*"

She held out a bunch of keys and an envelope. I recognized Mum's writing on the envelope – Miss Claire Masters, 8/14 rue Fleury, Neuilly-sur-Seine,

Paris, France. A line had been slashed through it and "Vicky" scribbled in its stead. The envelope hadn't even been re-sealed. Claire had sliced it open with her usual precision – me, of course, I just rip – and simply left it. Anyone could have taken out her note and read it. Mme Dastugue probably had. Not that it would have mattered; it didn't really tell one anything.

The note was short and urgent: "Dear Identikit, Sorry not here to meet you. Had to go off, last minute change of plan. Flat's all yours, see you soon! XXX Claire."

I frowned, as I trailed up the steep flight of stairs behind Jean-Guy. This was all most unlike the Claire I had known for seventeen years – well, longer than seventeen if you count the time we were embryos together. Claire is my *twin*. We can read each other like books. We may not be that close, but we understand each other through and through. I am the one who dashes off notes on the backs of old shopping lists (for that was what it was: tea, cheese, baguettes...); Claire is the one who writes properly on Basildon Bond. I am the one who has last-minute changes of plan; Claire was a Girl Guide and likes to be prepared.

"What does she say?" Jean-Guy had reached Flat 8 and was inserting one of the keys in the lock.

"Doesn't really say anything ... just says last-minute change of plan."

"What did I tell you? Gone off with a boyfriend!"

"Not necessarily a boyfriend," I muttered.

"What have you got against boyfriends?"

I hadn't got anything against boyfriends; I was just striving to make sense of my twin's unusual behaviour.

"I suppose it's possible she's gone somewhere with someone from her language school." I said it doubtfully, not fully convinced even now. "I know there was an American girl she once mentioned."

"Oh, you're such a spoilsport!" said Jean-Guy. He took the note from me. "Hm … she's not giving much away, is she? Supports my theory. She's gone off with a man!"

We turned it into a joke between us, speculating, as we left the flat and walked up the road to Jean-Guy's hotel, what Claire's unknown boyfriend could be like. Jean-Guy said he would be a tall dour Swede called Ingmar who brooded a lot and worked for UNESCO. I fancied him as a German – Herman the German. Herman would be eighteen-going-on-forty and would wear grey suits and gold rimless spectacles. We agreed that whether it was Ingmar or Herman he would be exceedingly earnest and have no sense of humour. We couldn't see Claire falling for anyone frivolous. (I still couldn't see her falling for anyone at all, but it was a fun game to play.)

The Hotel Fleury was only a couple of minutes

away from the flat. I was relieved to discover that in fact it was quite classy – lots of glass and chrome and luscious thick carpets. I wouldn't have liked to think that Jean-Guy was slumming it purely on account of me. The rest of the Company were billeted in a hotel near the Champs-Elysées, from where they could walk to the theatre. Jean-Guy said, "Who wants to be stuck with that crew? I have quite enough of them during the day and evening, thank you very much! I don't need to see their ugly mugs at breakfast as well," but I still felt he would secretly have preferred it and had only volunteered to keep an eye on me to please Auntie Vi and Mum. Jean-Guy is an extremely sociable type, and actually so am I. To tell the truth, if Claire wasn't going to be there I was already having second thoughts about staying in the flat. I hadn't bargained on being by myself.

At the theatre, in the corps' dressing-room, everyone was talking about the Butcher of the Bois. (That was how they were referring to him, the Butcher of the Bois, as if he were someone they knew personally.) It was extraordinary because as a rule the only things people talk about in dressing-rooms are things to do with ballet – gossip on the lines of who's going out with whom or who's getting all the best parts; general moans and groans about costumes – costumes that don't fit, costumes that don't flatter, costumes that are hell to dance in, costumes that stink of old sweat and body make-up; whinges about shoes – too hard/too soft/not enough of them; whinges about food, about getting fat, about going on a diet. Almost everything is a whinge. The affairs of the outside world simply don't figure. Not as a rule. One might almost be living on a different planet for all the notice that's taken. I mean quite honestly, if someone were to ask me who the Chancellor of the Exchequer was I wouldn't have an inkling; it just doesn't seem that important. But this Butcher thing had really got to people.

When I arrived, Marcia was reading out loud from *France Soir*, translating as she went. (Marcia isn't any more academically brilliant than the rest of us, it's just that she went to this posh convent school where they had to speak French at every mealtime.)

"*The body, which has not yet been identified, is that of a young woman believed to be in her late teens or early twenties. As with the previous two cases, it was found in a shallow grave in a quiet part of the Bois. Police said yesterday they believe this to be the work of a serial killer and are concerned that he could strike again. Th—*"

"Have they identified the first two yet?"

Marcia ran her eye down the page. "No. *The two previous victims remain unidentified.*"

"This is grotesque," moaned Suzie. "I begin to wish we'd never come!"

"Oh, don't be such a wimp." Marcia slapped the

paper down. "So long as we go round in a bunch we'll be all right."

"I can't go round in a bunch!" I wailed. "I'm stuck out at Neuilly!"

"Yes, but you've got Jean-Guy to keep an eye on you," said Carmen. "Nothing's going to happen to you while you're with him."

Jean-Guy was a comfort, I had to admit; but I still wished Claire hadn't chosen this particular time to go off and leave me.

After the run-through (which was dire, as usual – run-throughs in strange theatres always are) the Company Manager spoke to us. He, too, was talking about the Butcher of the Bois.

"I don't want any of you girls out on the streets after dark. OK? Always make sure you've got one of the guys with you, or go in a cab, two together. It may cramp your style, but there's no point in taking unnecessary risks."

When we finally left the theatre it was still light, it being the beginning of April and the evenings drawing out. Some of the kids were going off to eat together.

"Is Your Highness coming with us?" Marcia wanted to know. "Or is she –" her gaze flickered across to Jean-Guy, talking to Sergei (our ballet master) at the stage door – "is she dining in more exalted company?"

I wasn't quite sure myself, to tell the truth. Jean-

Guy had promised to keep an eye on me; he hadn't promised to tote me round Paris with him. But that, it seemed, was what he intended.

"Ready?" He cocked an eyebrow, taking it for granted that I was going with him.

"Wow!" breathed Carmen.

Marcia shook her head. "Don't get your hopes up," she muttered.

Over dinner that night (in a bistro where Jean-Guy was well known from previous visits) we discussed yet again where Claire could have gone and whom she could have gone with. We tried the Ingmar/Herman game, but somehow it didn't work as well as it had before.

"What's the matter?" said Jean-Guy, at last. "You're not worried about her, are you?"

Was I worried? Had little tendrils of doubt already started to worm their way in? On the face of it, there was no reason – her note had stated quite clearly, "See you soon."

"It's just that it's so out of character!"

"Paris makes people do things out of character."

"Well – yes. Maybe, but –" Jean-Guy didn't know Claire like I did. She was the last person on earth ever to act impulsively. I didn't believe that just being in Paris could alter someone's basic personality. "She didn't say anything to you?" I said.

"To me?"

"When you spoke to her."

"When I spoke to her?" Jean-Guy looked vague. "When did I speak to her?"

"I thought you always rang her, when you came over."

"Oh! Yes; I do, as a rule. I didn't bother this time, since we were going to be seeing her. She sounded perfectly OK the time before."

That had only been a fortnight ago; what could change in a fortnight?

"Don't forget," said Jean-Guy, "that she's *en vacances*. Term's finished. It's the holiday period as far as she's concerned."

"Ye-e-es ... but the idea was she was going to stay on in Paris and study."

My twin was dead set on being an air hostess. She'd set herself the task of speaking perfect French by the end of the year. (Being Claire, she was then going to move on to Spain and get perfect Spanish. Very methodical, is Claire.)

"Mum hoped she might be going home."

"Well, wherever she is, she can't have gone far. She's obviously planning on coming back while we're still here."

"I suppose so."

"It's what she said."

It *was* what she had said; I couldn't deny it.

"Look, why don't we have a word with Mme D? See if she knows anything. Claire might just have mentioned something to her. People do speak to concierges."

Not Claire, I thought.

Mme Dastugue wasn't too pleased at being hauled out of her cubby-hole at eleven o'clock at night. I suppose you couldn't blame her, though Jean-Guy did apologize and explain that I was concerned about my twin (at least I think that's what he did).

Mme Dastugue simply folded her arms over her low-slung bosoms and said "*Je n'en sais rien,*" which even I could translate as meaning "I know nothing about it (and couldn't care less)." When Jean-Guy pressed her further (he told me afterwards that he'd asked her whether she knew any of Claire's friends, whether she'd noticed if Claire were specially close to any particular one) she said huffily that she was not in the habit of spying on people, which as we subsequently discovered was a monstrous untruth. She spent whole hours at a time glued to the window, peering out through a chink in the net curtains, checking on who came and went.

"I expect you'll find," said Jean-Guy, "knowing Claire, that she's trying to ring you right now to check you got here OK."

It would have been in character, but the telephone wasn't ringing as we reached the flat and it still wasn't ringing by the time Jean-Guy had gone and I was undressing for bed. I stood for a few seconds on the balcony in my nightdress, gazing out at the lights of Paris, wondering how many times my twin must have done the same thing.

It was warm for the beginning of April, and quite stuffy up there, under the roof. Claire's flat was officially classed as a "studio flat", which meant in effect that it was a glorified bedsit, just one room with cooking facilities in the corner, plus bath and toilet.

Standing on a cupboard next to the cooking facilities (primitive) was a tiny refrigerator. I peered inside it, wondering if Claire had stocked up before she had gone wherever it was she had gone, but it seemed she had not so much stocked up as simply left behind, for the fridge was full of opened and half-consumed items – milk, butter, cheese, salami. I stared at it, thoughtfully. That wasn't like Claire, either. Methodical people don't go away and leave food to rot, or for their guests to clear up. I plucked out a carton of milk and smelt it. It smelt OK, so obviously Claire couldn't have been gone that long. We should have asked Mme Dastugue when she had left.

On a sudden inspiration, I flung open the wardrobe to see if I could discern what clothes she'd taken. It looked to me as if she hadn't taken very many – just jeans and T-shirts, and maybe a couple of blouses and skirts, was my guess, judging from the clothes left in there. It's odd when we're so unlike in character that Claire and I actually have a shared taste in clothes. We both go for the casual look rather than the dressed-up. But unless she'd come into a fortune (which I would have known about) there was no way she could have acquired more of a wardrobe than I was now looking at – which would seem to indicate either that she didn't intend being away for very long, or that she had flung stuff into a bag at the last minute and gone off in a rush. Or maybe both together.

It was a mystery; but I supposed it would come clear sooner or later.

I was really tired after all that travelling and rehearsing. I think I must have fallen asleep virtually the minute my head touched the pillow – yes, and that was another thing. The bed didn't have a clean sheet on it. I mean, the sheet wasn't dirty, but you could tell it had been slept on.

That wasn't like Claire, either; she was always most meticulous. This whole thing was really weird. I had even noticed that there were dirty dishes in the wash-basin. Claire, that paragon of all the virtues, leaving dirty dishes behind! (I investigated them next morning but they didn't yield any clues as to what her last meal might have been, whether breakfast or dinner.) I remember thinking, not without a certain sneaky satisfaction, that Mum would be sorely disappointed to have *two* daughters who were sluts – and then I must have fallen asleep, for that was the last thought I remember having.

I came to with a start what seemed like seconds later (it turned out in fact to be nearly an hour). I lay there rigid, wondering what had woken me. A full moon was shining through the skylight above my head. In the distance was the hum of traffic. And then I heard it, a sound which did not fit in with the general pattern of night-time sounds. A scraping, a sliding, somewhere on the roof.

I jerked upright, ears strained, every muscle tense. Suddenly I could no longer see the moon shining through the skylight. It had been blotted out by a large black shape.

Even as I looked at it, the shape moved. It moved across the skylight and the moon shone through once more, sending streams of silver cascading into the room.

And now the sound came again, that stealthy scraping and slithering across the roof – except that this time it was followed by a soft thud from somewhere directly outside.

I turned my head sharply towards the balcony. A scream rose to my lips and was stifled only because my throat was too tense to let it out. A dark shadow was lurking outside the double doors – the doors which I in my carelessness had left open.

I couldn't swear to it afterwards, but at the time I was almost certain it was the shadow of a man.

3

I don't think I ever moved so fast in my life. I am noted for the speed of my pirouettes, but the speed of my pirouettes is as nothing compared with the speed at which I leapt out of Claire's bed, shot across Claire's floor and dived through Claire's front door. Fortunately I retained just enough presence of mind to snatch up my dressing-gown and grab the keys off the table as I ran. A girl dashing through the midnight streets in her night-dress might have caused some comment, even in Paris.

It never occurred to me to bang on Mme Dastugue's door and get her to call the police. I mean, I couldn't speak the language for a start – *Au secours! Il y a un homme sur mon balcon!* Well, I *could* just about have managed it, I suppose, but the chances were she wouldn't have believed me. Most likely have written me off as some hysterical English girl who'd been reading too many horror stories about the Butcher of the Bois. But anyway, and more importantly, I wanted Jean-Guy.

The rue Fleury was empty (just as well). I tore up it to the hotel and burst in through the revolving door. If they were surprised at the sudden eruption of a barefoot girl wearing a blue Marks & Sparks dressing-gown and a polka dot nightdress, they showed it by no more than the faintest of raised eyebrows. Very cool, these Continentals.

Any French that I had deserted me completely.

"Jean-Guy Fontenille! Could you ring him for me, please?"

Of course they all spoke perfect English.

"I will try for you, Mlle, but I think he is not here."

Not there? Jean-Guy not there? Panic set in. That was something I hadn't bargained for! Where could he be? I'd assumed he was going straight back.

"*Sa clé —*"

His key was still hanging in its pigeon-hole where it had been placed when we had left the hotel together earlier in the day.

"I am sorry, Mlle. There is no reply from his room."

My heart plummeted. Now I felt foolish, as well

as scared. What was I going to do for the rest of the night?

"Does Mlle have some kind of problème? May one be of assistance?" (Pronounced *asseestons*.)

"I –"

At that moment, thank heavens, Jean-Guy arrived.

"Vicky! *Qu'est-ce qu'il y a?*"

I flung myself at him, babbling incoherently.

"Hang about, hang about!" With an arm round my shoulders, he led me over to one of the big plush sofas that dotted the reception area and sat me down. "*Bon! Alors*. Let's go through it again – but slowly. Slowly! You heard this noise –"

"I – heard this noise. And it – woke me up. And I – I saw the moon through the skylight, and then it – then it got blotted out and – then I saw it again and the – the thing that had been blotting it out had jumped on to the balcony and –"

"*Thing*," said Jean-Guy. "So it could have been an animal?"

"I –"

"A cat, for instance."

I shook my head, violently. "It was too big for a cat!"

"Are you sure? Things can be very deceptive at night – and some toms are enormous."

Now he was sowing the seeds of doubt. *Could* it have been a tom-cat? Was I really just some hysterical female who'd been listening to too many horror stories? I saw again the hunched black shape outside the balcony windows, and I could no longer be certain.

"Let's go back and take a look," said Jean-Guy. And then he glanced down at my feet and said, "Mother of God, she's not wearing any shoes!"

I blushed. I really was beginning to feel quite stupid.

"I rushed out without thinking," I mumbled.

"Sounds to me like a severe case of funk – come!" Before I knew what he was about, he had swung me up into his arms.

"It's all right," I protested. "I can walk! It's quite warm, it's –"

"Quite dangerous. You want to tread on broken glass and get a septic foot and not be able to dance?"

The threat of not being able to dance shut me up. Strangely enough – when you consider all the pain and general physical misery attached to it – dancers actually enjoy dancing. Most of us live to do nothing else. Meekly, therefore, I subsided into Jean-Guy's arms and allowed him to carry me out of the hotel (fantasizing as I went that some day we would be doing this on stage...)

"I hope they don't ring the newspapers," I said, noticing that this time the receptionist was closely monitoring our progress through the revolving door.

To this Jean-Guy only shrugged a shoulder and said *"Tant pis!* What would you have done if I hadn't come back?"

"I don't know." I said it sombrely. What would I have done? Wild horses wouldn't have got me back to the flat by myself. "Where –"

I was about to ask him where he had been, but abruptly thought better of it. Partly I wasn't sure that I wanted to know, partly I couldn't help feeling that it was really none of my business.

"It's all right!" Jean-Guy sounded amused. "You needn't get all censorious. He hasn't been up to anything Mummy wouldn't approve of... I just went for a stroll and had a coffee."

And why shouldn't he? Simply because I was ready for bed by eleven o'clock didn't mean that Jean-Guy had to be. He was used to late nights. It's difficult to unwind after a performance, so most dancers go off for a meal and get to bed somewhere in the early hours. I'd be doing it myself before the season was out.

We let ourselves in through the downstairs door – "Just as well you remembered to grab the keys!" said Jean-Guy. "I'm not a *total* cretin," I retorted – and crept up the stairs on tiptoe so as not to disturb the other tenants; or, I thought, any intruder who might be in the flat. As we reached Claire's door, I plucked nervously at Jean-Guy's sleeve.

"Suppose someone is in there?" I mouthed.

"Then I shall wallop them," Jean-Guy mouthed back.

He is strong, and extremely fit, so the chances are he would have done; but of course there was no one there. It had all, we decided, been the product of my fevered imagination. First night in Paris; horror stories doing the rounds; my twin disappeared...

"Not disappeared," Jean-Guy corrected me. "She just didn't think to tell us where she was going."

It came to the same thing as far as I was concerned, but I'd already made a big enough idiot of myself so I buttoned my lip and kept quiet. There was only one small point which bothered me: the balcony doors were closed.

"I'm sure I left them open," I said.

"Left them *open*?" Jean-Guy repeated it, incredulously. "You left your balcony doors *open*? And then you tell me you're not a total cretin?"

"Well, but it's hot," I muttered. "And we're three storeys up."

"Yes, and there's a flat roof directly above you and a madman roaming the streets." Jean-Guy strode across to the doors. They were not locked, it was true; but they were definitely closed.

"Closed is not good enough." Jean-Guy turned the key and shot the bolts both top and bottom. I still wondered how they had come to be shut when I had left them open. Jean-Guy seemed not to attach any significance to the fact.

34

"How open were they? Wide?"

"N-no. About ... like that." I held my finger and thumb a few centimetres apart. Jean-Guy looked at me. "I just wanted a bit of air," I pleaded.

He flipped his thumb towards the ventilator. "Have to make do with that. Better safe than sorry."

"Do you really think it could have been someone on the roof?"

"I don't think it *was* someone on the roof, but in theory it could have been. Do you want me to stay the night with you?"

My heart leapt in spite of myself. In spite of what Marcia had told me. The habits of a lifetime are very hard to break.

"I can kip down on the sofa," he said.

If Marcia hadn't gone and shattered my dreams, would I have been bold enough to point out that the bed was big enough for two? Only just, admittedly; but Claire and I had been going to manage.

Lamely I said: "I'll have the sofa, I'm smaller than you."

It was the least I could do. If one of us had to be uncomfortable, then it was only right it should be me, since I was the cause of it all with my too-vivid imagination. Jean-Guy tried to argue, but he didn't suggest we shared the bed. In the end I clinched matters by saying, "You're the big star. You oughtn't to have to sleep on a sofa."

"No, that's quite right," he said, as if struck

by the idea for the first time. "I oughtn't. I'm glad you thought of that! I don't believe in behaving like a gentleman, anyway ... we're all feminists now."

"Oh, absolutely," I said.

As a matter of fact – as a matter of sheer physical logistics – Jean-Guy couldn't possibly have slept on Claire's sofa. Even I found difficulty arranging my arms and legs. I woke up with a stiff neck and an ache in the small of my back, but if Jean-Guy hadn't been there I doubt I would have slept at all, so I suppose I shouldn't really have moaned. I did, all the same.

"I feel like a total wreckage," I said. I sketched a couple of pliés and groaned. "I think I've got arthritis of the spine."

Unfeelingly, Jean-Guy said, "You can't have pleasure without pain. Not in this business."

"I haven't had any pleasure!" I said. Scrunched into an S-bend on a sofa full of knobs and broken springs? Some pleasure that was!

"Look at it this way," said Jean-Guy. "When you're up there on stage performing physical contortions that rack every joint in your body, you are giving pleasure to thousands ... you're surely not telling me that isn't ample reward?"

I said, "OK for *some*, getting all the bouquets."

Jean-Guy made a priestly gesture. "Your turn will come, my child. Be patient."

36

I still couldn't help puzzling, as I flew round the flat collecting up tights, and shoes, and leotard, over the door that I had left open. Only a crack, I know; but how can a door close itself?

Jean-Guy had obviously been puzzling over it too, for all his nonchalant attitude of the night before.

"I think I've worked it out," he said. "You rushed off in a panic, right? Slammed the door behind you. Right? Created a vacuum." I looked at him, doubtfully. Science was never my strongest point, but then I don't think it was Jean-Guy's, either. "Sucked this one open with such force that it banged shut! How about that?"

"Mm ... maybe," I said.

"I'm telling you," said Jean-Guy. "Wham – bang – slam! That's your answer."

We didn't have time to try it out. We had to get off to class, and before that Jean-Guy needed to call at the hotel and collect his things. He left me in the restaurant eating croissants and went up to his room. While I was there the receptionist from last night came through. He gave me a very odd look. I suppose I couldn't really blame him. I just hoped he didn't try selling the story to the press – LEADING BALLET STAR CARRIES OFF GIRL IN NIGHTDRESS. Oh, they would have a field day!

In fact the papers that morning were full of more

gruesome details of the Butcher of the Bois' latest victim. Marcia was relaying them again in the dressing-room, reading from one of the sleaziest and most vulgar of the French tabloids. (You could tell it was sleazy and vulgar just by looking at it.) Everyone was hanging on her words, giving little squeals and squeaks and shudders of protest – but listening as hard as they could, nonetheless. I was listening with them. There was one part of me that didn't want to; but another part, I'm ashamed to admit, that almost relished the hideous titbits of information with which Marcia was regaling us.

I told Suzie, over a midday snack, the story of the night's events, and she said that if she were me she'd leave the flat and book into the hotel with the rest of them.

"I couldn't do that," I said. "I'd feel too stupid. I mean, it probably *was* only a cat."

"All the same," said Suzie.

"I've only got to remember to keep the doors locked." Which I most certainly would from now on. I didn't want a repeat performance, cat or no cat. After all, I couldn't keep running down the road in my dressing-gown in search of Jean-Guy; he might start to think I was pursuing him.

"Don't answer this if you don't want to," said Suzie, "but –" she glanced round, to make sure no one was listening – "are you and Jean-Guy –"

"What?" I said.

"Are you an item?"

I shook my head, pityingly. "Is that likely?"

"I don't see why not," said Suzie.

Suzie is actually a couple of months younger than I am; furthermore, she has had a very sheltered upbringing. In many ways she is still quite extraordinarily naïve.

"He looks upon me as a sister," I said. "And I," I added firmly, "look upon him as a brother."

I wasn't going to repeat Marcia's bit of scandal. I mean, not that Jean-Guy would have given two straws, in all probability; people don't, in the theatre, they just accept it as normal. But if Suzie couldn't see it for herself, then let her remain in blissful ignorance. She would learn.

"Does that mean he's up for grabs?" said Suzie. Quite forward, you note, in spite of her sheltered upbringing. "Is anyone free to try their luck?"

"Sure," I said; thinking that if Suzie dared throw herself at Jean-Guy I would personally dump a whole packet of itching powder down her leotard.

"Some hopes," sighed Suzie. "I guess you'd have to look like the lady Marcia to stand any sort of chance."

"Marcia?" I said, startled. What had she got that we hadn't? And then I thought of her – the lady Marcia, as Suzie scathingly referred to her. She was seriously gorgeous, no doubt about it. Legs that went on for ever, lustrous chestnut hair, seductive green eyes – *bone structure*. The only comfort was that Jean-Guy wouldn't look at her any more than he would look at us.

"I shouldn't worry about Marcia," I said.

It was Claire I was worried about, though for quite different reasons. Or perhaps worried wasn't as yet the right word. I was puzzled, I was curious – and yes, I did have the first faint twinges of uneasiness. But that was as far as it went. I hadn't yet started on the morbid thoughts.

For all that, at the end of the afternoon rehearsal I decided to venture down into the Métro and take myself back to the flat. I wanted to look again at my twin's note; see if I could glean any more from it than I had before.

The Métro was quite an adventure in itself, but really dead easy since the line went straight through from the Champs Elysées to Pont de Neuilly – not even a child could have got lost.

Back at the flat I looked in Claire's mail box – empty – nodded at Mme Dastugue, who was peering through her curtains, and ran up the three flights of stairs to the flat. It was most annoying! Claire's note was nowhere to be found. I tried to cast my mind back and think what I could have done with it, and then I remembered Jean-Guy taking it from me to read. What had Jean-Guy done with it? He told me afterwards that he had "just put it down somewhere – on the table, with the keys," but I hunted high and low and it never did turn up.

After searching fruitlessly for the better part of ten minutes I gave it up as a bad job and nerved myself to ring Mum, instead. I'd promised her I would, as soon as I had a spare moment, and I knew she'd be waiting anxiously by the telephone. The trouble was, I couldn't think what to say to her. Suppose she asked me about Claire? She would go into a flat spin if I told her that Claire wasn't here and I had no idea where she had gone. And then there was Dad to consider. Dad is more phlegmatic than Mum, he doesn't fuss and cluck as much, but he'd had a by-pass op. only a couple of months ago. He could do without the stress of Mum going to pieces on him.

In the end I cheated. I gabbled, "Mum? I'm here! I'm just ringing to let you know the plane didn't lose an engine or blow up in mid-air or anything. Jean-Guy's – yes, yes, the flat's fine! Jean-Guy – no, I haven't … no, I won't. I won't! I promise! Jean-Guy's hotel is just down the road, so – sorry? What did you say?"

"How is Claire?" is what Mum said.

"Help, look, Mum, I've really got to go! I've just seen the time. I was only calling to let you know I'm here. We've got a rehearsal at five, so – yes, I know! It is odd. But the stage is peculiar, it's got a very steep ramp and – what? Yes, I will! I'll be really careful. Anyway, I'll ring you again later. Give my love to Dad. 'Bye!"

I felt bad about cutting her off like that, but what else could I do? (Afterwards, some time afterwards, I thought that maybe I'd been wrong. Maybe I ought to have told her the truth, for suppose something dreadful had happened? Claire wasn't just my twin, she was Mum's daughter, and probably closer to Mum than she was to me. On the other hand, I consoled myself, why give a person nightmares when there was probably nothing in the least to worry about? That was what Jean-Guy kept saying.)

I wasn't in any particular rush – the stage did have a steep ramp, but we were all supposed to have got used to that yesterday. No extra rehearsal had been called; I had time on my hands. Still, I didn't fancy the idea of stuffing in the flat. Not much point coming to Paris and not seeing anything of it. I decided to be brave, and go and have a coffee on the Champs Elysées all by myself.

I picked up the keys and went trolling back downstairs. Mme Dastugue peered at me again through her curtains. I waved at her and smiled but she didn't smile back. I guess her face might have cracked had she tried it.

As I opened the main door to the street I almost bumped into a young man who was on the point of pressing one of the bells. (Claire's bell, as it turned out.)

"Oops!" I said. "Sorry!" And then, remembering which country I was in: *"Excusez-moi!"*

He looked at me and did a double-take.

"You must be Claire's twin," he said.

4

"Yes."

I stopped and turned. Someone who knew Claire! He was about Jean-Guy's age, i.e. twenty-two; cropped blond hair, a sprinkling of freckles, wide-apart eyes, bluey-grey, partly hidden behind a pair of incongruous horn-rimmed spectacles. I say incongruous because he had this fresh outdoor-life complexion as if he spent every weekend on the football field or hanging upside down over the sides of yachts, whereas horn-rimmed spectacles always create this solemn, studious image. At least, they do for me. Also, these were very *large* horn-rimmed spectacles and he had this rather short stubby nose, so that they kept slipping down to the end of it and almost going over the edge. Even as we stood there he was busy shunting them up with the middle finger of his right hand.

"I'm Vicky," I said.

"I know." He smiled, shyly and engagingly. "Claire's told me about you. I'm Tracey."

He had just the faintest of transatlantic accents. American? Canadian? I can never tell the difference.

"You don't know where Claire is, do you?" I said.

"No." His face clouded over. "I was hoping you might."

"No! I was supposed to be staying with her. She was supposed to be here. Then when I arrived I found this note saying she'd had a sudden change of plan. She didn't say where she was going, she didn't say when she was coming back ... I don't even know when she went!"

"She wasn't here Sunday evening, I can tell you that."

Sunday; the day before we arrived.

"I called round and I couldn't raise any reply. I tried again later, I tried telephoning, I tried the concierge —"

"Mme Dastugue. She was the one who gave us Claire's note. But all she says when you ask her anything is *je n'en sais rien* and scowls."

"I know; she's really grim. She won't open her mouth for less than fifty francs."

I glanced back towards the apartment building.

"You think she actually knows something? You

think if we gave her money —"

"Uh-uh." He shook his head. "Not in this instance. I already tried. The thing is, I'm — I'm getting a bit concerned."

"Me, too," I said. I wasn't sure, before, that I had been; but now that I seriously stopped to consider it, I knew that I was.

"Could we go and have a coffee some place, do you think? Or do you have to —" he shunted his glasses back up — "do you have to get off?"

"Not for a while. I've got about half an hour."

"So shall we find somewhere?"

I suggested we made it somewhere near the theatre so that I wouldn't be fussed about time. He didn't know which theatre we were appearing at, nor even that I was a dancer, which meant Claire couldn't have told him all that much about me. I can't say I was surprised, Claire has never been a fan of the ballet. Thinking about it, I was mildly amazed that she had bothered mentioning me at all. The last thing I would ever do when faced with an attractive male is volunteer the information that I have a pea-in-the-pod look-alike for a sister.

I said so to Tracey, as we parked ourselves under a big stripey umbrella on the Champs-Elysées.

"You don't like being a twin?" he said.

He sounded almost hurt by the discovery. People often are. I guess it ruins their illusions. They like to think of twins being all in all to each other, telepathically attuned, transmitting every little ache and pain, every joy, every sorrow. Lots are, I daresay; but Claire at this moment was transmitting absolutely zilch. She could have been anywhere on the face of the earth.

"I do think," I said, "that it would be far nicer for both of us if we were just ordinary sisters. It gets us really mad at times, the way people keep expecting us to do everything the same. Just because we look alike," I said, warming to my theme, "doesn't mean we *are* alike. We're actually two quite separate people. But they just don't give us a chance."

"Yeah. I guess it's something you could get pretty sick of." Tracey nodded sympathetically – and then cavalierly went ahead and ordered two black coffees without even consulting me.

"You see?" I leapt on it. "You take it for granted I'm going to have the same as Claire!"

"Oh!" He clapped a hand to his forehead. "Hey, I'm sorry! I should have asked. Let me –"

"It's all right," I said. "As it *happens*, I like my coffee black."

That was one of the strange – and infuriating! – anomalies. In spite of being such determinedly different people, Claire and I not only shared the same dress sense but the same tastes in food. It was something we couldn't help. We kept trying to educate ourselves in different directions, but there's not very much that you can do about your genes.

"When we were young," I said, "it used to drive us practically demented. We got so we almost couldn't stand the sight of each other. We used to hatch murder plots … I remember once I put dandelion juice in Claire's milk 'cause I thought it might be poisonous. And then one time she stuffed my fingers in the mincer and was going to mince them. I threatened to do her for that. And I did, too! I whacked her on the head with a wooden spoon. Our mum used to say it was like having two infantile psychopaths in the house. But it's all right now," I said, in case he was taking it too seriously – he was staring at me in a kind of appalled fascination, eyes open wide behind his horn-rimmed specs. "We're quite fond of each other now. In fact," I said, "we're very fond of each other. I was really looking forward to seeing her again."

"Yeah." Tracey nodded. "She was really looking forward to seeing you."

"Which just makes it all the harder to understand. It's not like her to do things on impulse."

"Or to let people down?"

I blushed. I actually felt quite ashamed for my twin's behaviour.

"*Definitely* not to let people down. Jean-Guy says Paris can do strange things to you, but –"

"Who's Jean-Guy?"

So! Claire hadn't mentioned Jean-Guy. Well, that figured. She has never been as close to him as I have. Basically (I suspect) she considers male dancers to be frippery, flibbertigibbet kinds of people.

"Jean-Guy Fontenille," I said; but of course it didn't mean anything. Your average male has just about heard of Nijinsky. For the rest – Nureyev, Baryshnikov, Erik Bruhn, Roland Petit, Jean-Guy Fontenille ... forget it!

"Jean-Guy's an old friend of the family," I said. "His mum and ours used to be in a dance troupe together. Now he's a premier danseur with the Barbican."

I waited for the usual male reaction, raised eyebrows and slight downturn of the lips – and that's when they're being *polite* – but all Tracey said was, "Is that the same company you're in? Are you a ballerina?"

I shook my head, vigorously. "I only joined a few months ago. I'm still in the corps."

"I'm sure you won't be for long," he said.

It was really sweet: he blushed as he said it. Being American (or Canadian) he came across with this immediate impression of being all laid-back and cool, but you could tell that underneath he was quite shy. I liked that. I hardly ever get to meet any shy people. It made a nice change.

"How long have you known Claire?" I said.

"Not that long. Just a couple of weeks or so. But –" he blushed some more – "we were really getting it together; you know? Or at least, I thought we were."

"Where did you meet?" I was intrigued – and perhaps, if the truth were told, just the tiniest bit jealous. How come my superior-minded twin (she had *never* had any patience with all my yearnings and passions) had managed to find someone this attractive? OK, so he didn't have the exotic good looks of Jean-Guy, nor Jean-Guy's lithe suppleness, in fact just the opposite, he was quite stocky and solid, not really my type at all; but for all that I had this darting twinge of jealousy. (I think what it was, I am so used to the rude, flamboyant ways of theatre people that anyone who is at all hesitant just knocks me out.)

"We met –" he gave a little apologetic laugh, as if about to confess to something shameful. "We met like this, having coffee."

"Aha!" I couldn't resist it. "You mean, Claire was a *pick up*?"

I was only teasing, of course, but he blushed quite painfully.

"No, no! It wasn't like that at all. She was by herself, and all the tables were full, so I asked if I could sit down, and she said yes, and – well! We just got talking."

Claire? Just got *talking?* Maybe Paris did do strange things to people!

"We went out a few times – a couple of

50

nightclubs, a couple of shows. I was with her Saturday; everything seemed fine. I said I'd see her Sunday. I called round Sunday and – she wasn't there. So, OK, at first I think maybe she's just standing me up –"

"Claire wouldn't do that!" I said. You have to give people their due. Claire was utterly one hundred per cent reliable. If she'd arranged to meet, she would meet. At least, that's what I'd always thought.

"You hadn't quarrelled or anything?"

"Not one cross word had ever passed between us. That's why I just couldn't understand it."

No; I couldn't understand it, either. This whole pattern of behaviour was as unlike Claire as anything I could think of.

"Even if for some reason she'd decided she didn't want to see you again, she would have told you. She wouldn't just not turn up."

"Well, that's what I figured. She just didn't seem that kind of girl. She seemed too – too straight. You know?"

I nodded; I did know. Claire *was* straight. Straight up and down. Straight as a die. No nonsense.

"Look," I said, "I really have to be going, it's our opening night. I don't want to be late. But can we talk again?"

I won't deny that I found him attractive, but it wasn't just that; it was the fact that he knew Claire.

"Could we meet after the show, maybe?" He suggested it almost – I was going to say timidly, but that's not quite the right word. *Modestly*. Unlike Jean-Guy, he obviously was not accustomed to women grasping eagerly at every least suggestion he made.

"After the show would be fine," I said. And then, on impulse: "Why don't you come along and see it?" I knew that Jean-Guy, as one of the principals, had a couple of free tickets that he hadn't used. I didn't think he would mind giving one to a friend of Claire's.

"I'd love to," said Tracey, "but unfortunately I'm on early shift."

He explained that he worked for an American bank, in their computer room. Sometimes he was on night shift, sometimes on early shift. Early shift meant he had to be there from six o'clock through till midnight.

"But I can get away by half eleven, no problem. We cover for each other." Again, he gave me that shy smile; with just a hint of wickedness. "It's one of the perks of the job ... no one there to oversee us."

"You mean you skive off," I said. "That's what I used to do at school. They got so sick of it in the end they let me leave and go to dancing school instead."

"I don't do it all the time." He was anxious that I should know. "That would be like cheating. But just now and again, when things are quiet, I figure it can't do much harm."

"No, and we do need to talk," I agreed, "because honestly, all this isn't in the least like Claire."

"So I'll see you outside the theatre. Eleven-thirty?"

"That would be fine."

"Could I take you for a meal, maybe? Would you feel like eating after doing a show?"

"Eating," I assured him, "is what I always feel like doing after a show!"

I was the last to arrive in the dressing-room. Not that I was late, but the rest were already hard at it, pulling on tights, scragging back hair, applying make-up.

"There you are!" said Suzie, as if I had been lost and had suddenly re-surfaced. "Jean-Guy was asking if anyone had seen you."

"Poor diddums," crooned Marcia. "He thought the nasty Butcher man had got her."

"No one knew where you were," said Suzie.

"I just popped back to the flat to see if Claire had turned up."

"Had she?"

I shook my head. "No, but I bumped into a boy-friend of hers. He's taking me out for a meal after the show."

"Hey! Wow!" Marcia was viciously hammering at one of her point shoes, trying to soften the block.

"That was quick work! How to half inch your sister's boyfriend in one easy move."

"I'm not half inching him!" I lobbed a screwed-up chocolate wrapper at her. "I'm trying to find out what's got into Claire."

All the dressing-room knew that my twin sister had mysteriously gone off. The general consensus was that she was having a mad passionate affair and had run away to be with her lover – a married man, in all probability.

I hadn't believed it before, when Jean-Guy and I had been joking about Ingmar and Herman; I believed it even less now that I had met Tracey. The thought of him chatting up my twin sister over a cup of coffee wasn't so very mind-boggling now that I had grown used to the idea, for if ever Claire were going to have a boyfriend Tracey was exactly the sort I would have picked for her – nice-looking without being in any way remarkable, introverted rather than extrovert (Claire can't stand theatricals for that very reason. She says we are all screamers) and safely employed in a steady sensible job, working with computers. I could see Claire and Tracey as a couple. What I couldn't see was my twin in the throes of a mad passionate affair, especially not with a married man.

On my way down to the stage to warm up, I bumped into Jean-Guy.

"Where have you been?" he said.

"I went back to the flat. I wanted to have another look at Claire's note."

That was when I told him I hadn't been able to find it and he claimed to have put it on the table with the keys. I also told him about Tracey and how he was going to take me out for a meal, thinking he would be pleased because it would free him to go off and do his own thing without worrying about me and what I was up to. I couldn't honestly believe that someone in Jean-Guy's position wanted to spend the whole of his time in Paris nursemaiding one of the lowliest forms of Company life – especially as he could remember me when I'd still been messing my nappies. *Not* very romantic.

To my surprise, he not only wasn't pleased but actually blew up in a rage. ("Unstable." I could almost hear Claire saying it. It's another of the accusations she raises against the theatrical profession. We are all screamers, we are all neurotics, we all have kingsize egos and we are all *unstable*.)

"What do you mean, he's taking you out for a meal? You don't know the guy from Adam! He turns up on the doorstep, claiming to know Claire –"

"He does know Claire. He knew who I was, too."

"So what?"

"So Claire told him is so what. She'd told him I was going to stay there. The minute he saw me, he said, 'You must be Claire's twin.'"

"Big deal! So he said you must be Claire's twin."

"Yes."

Jean-Guy gave me a decidedly smouldering look.

"I don't see what the problem is," I said. "He's Claire's *boy*friend."

"So if he's Claire's boyfriend, he won't mind me tagging along, will he?"

I knew that it was just another of his nurse-maiding duties. If there hadn't been a madman roaming the streets, he wouldn't have turned a hair at the thought of me going out to dinner with my twin sister's boyfriend. He would have been only too relieved to be rid of me.

I couldn't help feeling just a little bit happy, all the same.

5

For opening night, we performed *Giselle*. *Giselle* is one of my favourite ballets of all time, especially when Jean-Guy is dancing the lead. He is a truly great Albrecht.

(In case anyone thinks that is just me being prejudiced, I will quote from an eminent French ballet critic: "*L'Albrecht de Jean-Guy Fontenille était tout simplement superbe*" – which I should think anyone could translate.)

I loved to watch him in the second act. This is the "white act" where Giselle, dead of a broken heart (Albrecht has two–timed her) has joined the ranks of the Wilis – a bunch of power-crazed feminists out to get men, according to Jean-Guy. In point of fact they are all Betrayed Maidens and the only men they are out to get are those who have played fast and loose and therefore deserve it, if you want my opinion.

Albrecht is duly hunted down and forced to dance until he drops, except that that silly ninny, Giselle, goes and intercedes on his behalf and actually manages to save him (I wouldn't!) which gives magnificent scope for someone like Jean-Guy to perform gravity-defying leaps and spins while at the same time managing to convey that he is on the point of collapse, e.g. by picturesquely crumpling every now and again at Giselle's feet and having to be gently raised up and given the strength to go on. Great stuff!

With some Albrechts I get so fidgety on behalf of poor ill-used Hilarion ("A Woodcutter") who loved Giselle long before the two-faced Albrecht came on the scene and ousted him, that I really resent it when Giselle pulls out all the stops to save the one and not the other – because she doesn't lift a finger when the pack close in on Hilarion.

With Jean-Guy, though I still thought it was unfair, I was sufficiently heart-wrenched by his remorse to accept that life is like that. It *is* unfair.

It was unfair, for instance, that Tracey had to wear glasses and that seen close up, over dinner, his skin wasn't quite as fresh as I had first thought but was minutely pitted with the scars of what I suppose must have been acne.

Jean-Guy, needless to say, never suffered from acne. Jean-Guy never has to wear glasses, even for driving. Jean-Guy has pretty well everything going for him that you can possibly think of – health, wealth, looks, talent. What more could you ask? He could get any woman he wanted (assuming he wanted). I couldn't see Jean-Guy fretting and breast-beating because someone appeared to have thrown him over.

I felt sorry for Tracey, being landed with Jean-Guy. Jean-Guy paid his way, of course – in fact he paid for me as well – but I think what Tracey was really looking for was a heart-to-heart with someone who was prepared to be sympathetic. He was not only basically shy, but also, I realized, desperately unsure of himself. Even now he wasn't convinced that it might not have been something which he had said or done that had driven Claire away.

Whereas I would have listened and made soothing noises and done my best to reason his fears out of existence, Jean-Guy treated them as ludicrous and preposterous.

"Why should it be something you've done? Unless you have some very peculiar habits you haven't told us about."

Tracey blushed so deep a crimson that I actually felt embarrassed for him. He shunted his spectacles up his nose.

"I haven't any p-peculiar h-habits!"

"So why think it's anything to do with you?"

Jean-Guy just doesn't seem to understand that there are some men in the world who possess a quality known as *modesty*. Whenever he meets up with it, it seems to baffle and irritate him. I find it quite becoming, myself. Not that Jean-Guy, you understand, is particularly bombastic or boastful, in fact he can even be quite humble where his dancing is concerned; but it has to be said that in his relationships with other people he knows the value of his own charm, or at any rate tends to take it for granted.

Tracey, by contrast, needed reassuring. It seemed to me that he had too low an opinion of himself. Quiet, self-effacing charm can be just as effective as the sort that leaps out and hits you between the eyes. He had obviously never grasped the fact.

Sitting there opposite him, seeing that puckered frown starting to gather on his forehead, I felt a sudden urge to defend him.

"It's worrying," I said; and I looked quite crossly at Jean-Guy. "It *is* worrying, where she's gone."

"Why? Why should it worry you?" Jean-Guy hunched his shoulders up to his ears and spread his hands in exaggerated Gallic fashion. (He looked like an ad for Gauloises.) "She's not a child; she can go where she likes. Besides, she left you a note."

"Yes, which I can't find!"

"So what do you want to find it for? You've already read it."

"I wanted to have another look at it. See if it gave me any clues. Check it really was Claire's handwriting."

Jean-Guy clicked his tongue, impatiently.

"You see, what worries me —" Tracey leaned forward. He shunted his glasses with the middle finger of his right hand. "I don't want to be alarmist in any way, but I happen to know there was some guy that was pestering her."

"Pestering her?" I, too, leaned forward. "Pestering her how?"

"I don't exactly know how, but I do know she was pretty sick of it. She said to me one time she wanted to be out of the flat in case he called round. She said she didn't like to be on her own with him any more."

"You mean … in case he was violent?" I said.

Tracey shook his head. "She didn't say. But I know she didn't want him round any more."

"And you've no idea who he was?"

"She never gave me any name. But I guess she must have known him some while."

"What makes you guess that?" said Jean-Guy.

"Uh – well." Tracey took off his glasses and began to wipe at them with a napkin. "She said on one occasion something about – about him thinking he could just come and go. 'As if he owns me.' So I have to assume it was some guy she was pretty intimate with."

This was a fresh puzzle. Who could Claire possibly be intimate with? She had only been in Paris eight months. Eight months might be time enough for me to reach that stage with someone, but not Claire. And of course she'd never mentioned anything in her letters home, but then she wouldn't.

"Lover's tiff," said Jean-Guy.

"Well, it was certainly all over," said Tracey, "I can tell you that."

"If you want my opinion –" Jean-Guy stretched out, in lordly fashion – "we're making needles out of haystacks."

"Mountains out of molehills," I said. It's funny, but just now and again he does get his idioms in a muddle. I rather like it: it cuts him down to size. Makes him less godlike and more endearing.

"Whichever you prefer." He waved a careless hand. "Needles out of haystacks, mountains out of molehills –"

Tracey finished wiping his glasses and re-settled them on his nose.

"You think I'm making a fuss about nothing?"

"I think she's only been gone a couple of days –"

"Three!" Tracey was quick to correct him.

"OK; three. She's only been gone three days, she left a perfectly coherent note, there's no reason on earth why she shouldn't decide she wants to dash off and see another part of France –"

"There is when she'd arranged to see Tracey on Sunday evening," I said.

"So maybe she forgot. Maybe someone suddenly said, 'Hey, how about we jump on a train and go off to Switzerland for the weekend,' and that was that. Pfui! Off she went. People do things like that. You'd be surprised. You'll probably get a postcard first thing tomorrow morning with a picture of Lake Lucerne."

I turned to Tracey, slumped despondently on his chair.

"If I do," I said, "I'll ring you immediately."

"You have my number? Let me give you my number!"

He handed me a card which said "TransAmerican Bank". He didn't have his name printed on it, but I suppose he was still too young for that. (I have to keep reminding myself that other occupations – *sensible* occupations – are not like ballet, where you're middle-aged by twenty-five and over the hill by thirty.) He wrote it on there for me, Tracey van den Hul, and put his extension, 212.

"Or here's my home number, if you need to get me during the day."

"And if you hear anything," I said, "like if she rings you or anything, you'll let me know?"

"I will, immediately," he said. He shunted his spectacles. "Can I call a cab and escort you folks some place?"

I loved the thought of being escorted, but Jean-Guy plainly didn't fancy the idea. He said quite unnecessarily curtly that we could make our own way back. Tracey reddened, so that I felt quite ashamed of Jean-Guy.

"You didn't have to treat him like dirt," I said, as we bowled off in a cab of our own.

"The guy's a neurotic."

"Just because he's worried?"

"If he's that worried, why doesn't he go to the police?"

I was silent for a while. "You don't think we ought?" I said.

"And tell them what? That your nearly eighteen-year-old sister stood up her boyfriend and decided to go walkabout and didn't inform you where she was going? There's no law against it! What do you think the police are likely to do?"

Nothing; I knew he was right. They would say there were "no grounds for suspicion". You couldn't count as a missing person someone who had gone off of their own free will (assuming that Claire had, which at that point I still was).

"What about this man that was pestering her?" I said.

"Girls are always going on about guys pestering them. I seem to remember a time when you were going on about someone pestering you ... some poor harmless youth who just wanted you to go to a disco with him and you got Aunt Liz to tell him you'd flown off to China?"

"That was Jimmy Blakemore; he was mad."

"You said he was a pest."

"Well, he was. He wouldn't ever take no for an answer."

"There's a lot of us about," said Jean-Guy. "It doesn't mean we're all raving nutters. Most of us are just pathetic harmless nuisances."

What did he know about it? Since when had anyone ever said no to him?

I had a call at the theatre next day. It was Tracey, eager to hear if I'd had any sort of communication from Claire. I said that I hadn't, and he said neither had he.

"But I've found something out."

"What's that?" I said.

"I just called round to speak to the concierge. I asked her about this guy … the one that Claire didn't want to be on her own with?"

"Mm." I nodded encouragement down the telephone.

"I asked if she had any idea who he might be, or whether she'd ever noticed him visiting with Claire."

"And had she?"

"She didn't know who he was but she said there was a guy used to come by. She claimed never to have gotten a good look at him. All she could tell me, he was tall and dark and used to let himself in, which meant he had his own key – which according to her, he wasn't supposed to have."

"Had his own key?"

I didn't like the sound of that. Why would Claire give her key to anyone? I mean, she'd given it to me for obvious reasons; but to some stranger? It suddenly struck me that maybe I didn't know my twin sister quite as well as I thought.

"I know it's not a lot to go on," said Tracey.

It wasn't anything to go on, unless we could find out who the tall dark stranger was. (The thought occurred to me, unbidden – and I wished that it hadn't – that as yet the police had no idea of the Butcher's physical characteristics. No one, as far as we knew, had survived to tell the tale.)

"How did you get her to tell you even that much?" I said.

"Oh, I – uh –" Tracey gave a little embarrassed laugh – "I greased her palm."

The infamous *pourboire* that Claire had complained of.

"Fifty francs?"

"You've got it."

I wondered what, if anything, she would give away for five hundred.

"While I've got you on the phone –" He suddenly went all bashful; I could hear it, in his voice – "I'm coming to see you dance tonight."

"Really? You managed to get a ticket?"

"I was lucky, they had a return."

"I hope you like it," I said.

"It's got to be better than staying home and brooding over Claire."

"Is that what you're doing?"

"I can't help it! I keep wondering where she is, whether she's OK —" He broke off. "You wouldn't care to come and eat with me after the show, would you? I have to be on duty at midnight, but I could always swing it for an extra half hour."

I said that of course I would and that I would meet him at the stage door. What else could I say? As I pointed out to Jean-Guy, when he exploded for the second time, this was Claire's *boy*friend. He was justifiably upset. As her twin sister, I felt almost duty bound.

"Are you your sister's keeper? Tell him I'd already booked us a table somewhere. If he wants he can tag along, it's up to him."

I was torn between a strong feminist resentment at being bullied and an equally strong, and hopelessly non-feminist, desire to cave in meekly and do whatever I was told. After a bit of flouncing and petty rebellion, I caved in. I wouldn't have done had it been anyone other than Jean-Guy.

We danced *Coppélia* that night. *Coppélia* is the story of Swanhilda, who catches her boyfriend Franz conducting a flirtation with the beautiful girl who sits on the balcony of the house owned by old Dr Coppélius. She and her friends break into the house in search of the girl and discover her to be only a doll. Franz had been flirting with a doll! What a laugh!

It's a light-hearted ballet, quite different from *Giselle*, and frankly I have never thought that Jean-Guy is ideal as Franz. I always see Franz as being open and fresh-faced, very much the boy next door – a bit like Tracey, without the horn rims. Jean-Guy is far too dark and sultry-looking. Still it was fun, and I hoped that Tracey enjoyed it and that it took his mind off Claire for a while.

I don't think he was too happy at being asked to "tag along". After last night I couldn't really blame him, but this time as it happened Jean-Guy was on his best behaviour. He sympathized with Tracey's concern, soothed his fears, explained how Paris "did strange things to people" and advised him just to sit back and await her return.

"Then you can demand explanations … I'd demand some if she were mine!"

Tracey went off, still looking rather dejected, to do his night shift in the computer room, while Jean-Guy and I took a cab back to Neuilly. Jean-Guy insisted on coming up with me, to see me safely inside. He closed the door of the flat and stood leaning for a moment with his back against it.

"Victoria," he said.

He never called me Victoria; it sounded strange coming from his lips. He was looking at me oddly, as well. Almost ... almost as if he were weighing things up. Coming to some sort of decision.

"Yes?" I said, trying to sound all bright and chirpy.

He took a step forward, resting his hands on my shoulders, gazing down at me in brooding fashion. I had never noticed before that Jean-Guy can look quite menacing. The thought ran through my brain: he'll make a wonderful von Rothbart when he's too old to dance Siegfried...

"Vicky —" His hands slid either side of my neck. I felt a tingling sensation go prickling down my spine and wasn't quite sure whether it was pleasurable or not.

"W-what?" I said.

"Nothing. It's all right. It'll keep." He dropped his hands abruptly, jerked open the door and went springing off down the stairs. At the bottom of the first flight he turned and called up to me: "Put that chain on!"

I did so, wondering as I slid it into place what he had been about to do, or say. I had never felt uncomfortable with Jean-Guy before.

It wasn't until some time after he had gone — I'd already washed and undressed and was on the point of climbing into bed — that I remembered: I hadn't told him about Claire giving her key to the tall dark stranger. I still felt a bit edgy about that, in spite of the chain being on the door.

I put through a call to his room at the hotel, but of course he wasn't back yet. I'd forgotten his French habit of going to sit in a bistro till the small hours – or perhaps it wasn't a French habit so much as a dancer's habit. It's relatively easy, when you're still only a member of the corps, to relax afterwards and go to bed. You don't have to come down from the high of having given a solo performance, nor do you spend half the night going over it in your mind, re-dancing it step by step, mentally noting all those areas where you might have done better.

I checked the balcony doors were shut and locked, double-checked the chain was securely in place, jumped into bed and fell asleep – and spent half *my* night dreaming of tall dark strangers creeping up the stairs with butchers' knives in their hands. It wasn't at all restful.

Next evening, someone brought a copy of *France Soir* into the dressing-room. It was then I saw the headline which made the blood run chill in my veins:

BUTCHER STRIKES AGAIN...

6

Another body found in Bois de Boulogne.

The ghouls were already gathered, badgering Marcia to do a translation for them.

"Go on!" Josie Howatt, the one who had brought the paper in, thrust it at her. "Tell us the worst."

Suddenly, I didn't want to know. I left the room and fled down the stairs to where the soloist and principals hung out. Jean-Guy, of course, being a leading dancer, had a room to himself. I thumped at the door with my fist. It was his dresser, Dennis, who opened it.

"I need to speak to Jean-Guy!" I said.

He raised his eyebrows, one after another, very slowly. Humble members of the corps did not, as a rule, go barging into the premier danseur's room when he was in the middle of preparing for a performance.

"Vicky?" Jean-Guy was sitting at his dressing-table, stripped to the waist, applying make-up. He spoke to me through the mirror. "What's the problem?"

I shot into the room, falling dramatically to my knees at his side.

"They've found another one!"

"Another what?"

"Another body!"

He leaned in closer to the mirror. "All the more reason for not going out to dinner with strange men."

"Jean-Guy, I'm worried," I said.

"No need; just stick with me, you'll be fine. I said I'd keep a watch out for you —" carefully, he outlined an eye with eyeliner — "and that is what I intend doing, no matter how much lip you give me."

That was a reference to my flouncing rebellion of the night before. He was wilfully misinterpreting; he knew perfectly well it wasn't myself I was worried for. Did I really have to spell it out? In front of Dennis?

"Jean-Guy," I said, urgently, "you don't think —"

"What?"

He was evidently determined to make things as difficult as possible. (He explained afterwards that he didn't want me going to pieces before a performance, and all for no reason. At least, for no reason as he saw it. But I wouldn't have gone to pieces! He was far more likely to make me do so by being deliberately obtuse.)

"Listen," he said; and for the first time he swivelled his eyes away from the mirror to look directly at me. "Watch my lips ... *there is nothing to worry about*."

"But –"

"We'll talk it out later. Over dinner. OK?"

He didn't sound unsympathetic, but he did make it very clear that now was not the moment. I had no option but to leave. Jean-Guy is not more than averagely a prima donna – I mean, all big stars are to some extent, and Jean-Guy could throw a tantrum with the best of them, but generally speaking he is not what I would call unapproachable. On the other hand, when his tone indicates "Do I make myself clear?" it is wisest not to stay and argue with him.

I trailed back up the stairs to the concrete barracks that was the corps' dressing-room. (Dennis gave me such a sour look as I left. I don't think he approves of "his stars" hobnobbing with the rubbish. He likes to think that some of their glory rubs off on him. The likes of me only tarnish it.)

"Did you hear?" wailed Suzie, as I seated myself at the dressing-table next to hers. "There's been another one!"

"I know; I saw." I desperately didn't want the gory details, not before I had to go on and dance, but of course people can never resist it. Ghastly though it is, murder seems to hold a curious fascination for the human mind.

"Police," intoned Marcia, reading from the paper, "are appealing for members of the public to come forward. They have still been unable to identify any of the bodies."

"They think this latest one might be English," hissed Suzie. "She was wearing Marks & Sparks underwear. Though of course," she added hastily, "that isn't necessarily anything to go by. Not these days. They have Marks & Spencer everywhere. Don't they, Marcia? Don't they have Marks & Spencer everywhere?"

"There's one in Paris," said Josie. "A big one."

"Probably more than one."

"Well, this is it." Suzie's relief was pitiable to behold. "Goodness knows why they should think someone's English just because they're wearing Marks & Spencer underwear! I bet even the President of France, I bet even he wears Marks & Spencer Y-fronts!"

"Who is the President of France, anyway?" I said; but nobody knew and nobody cared. They were all of a twitter over the latest gruesome discovery.

"One metre 65," said someone, craning over Marcia's shoulder. "How tall's 1.65?"

Nobody knew that, either, but Marcia obligingly worked it out.

"About 5′ 5″."

"One metre 65 tall and weighs about 54 kilos."

"8½ stone."

"Ugh! Fat!"

It would have been fat, for a dancer. I am 5′ 5″ and only weigh 7st. 10lb. (or 7st. 8lb., on a good day). But for normal people, 8½ stone was nothing. It was what Claire probably weighed. You didn't really notice when people had clothes on. It's only tights and leotards that are so revealing.

"They say it's probably been there for about three or four days judging by the state of the body." Marcia was scrutinizing the paper again, eager to bring me up to date. "*According to the detective in charge of the case, she is the latest but almost certainly not the last victim. 'We are dealing with a psychopath and must expect him to strike again.'*"

Suzie, behind my back, was making frantic signals to Marcia to keep quiet. (I could see her, quite clearly, in someone else's mirror.) Marcia carried on regardless. I think she is what is known as thick-skinned. Hide like a hippopotamus.

"*This was a particularly br—*"

"Do we really need all this?" I said quickly. My hands were beginning to shake as I applied my make-up.

"I thought you wanted to hear?"

"Not before a performance of *Sylphides*," pleaded Suzie.

"Anyway," said Carmen, "we've heard it all once."

"Vix hasn't! She wasn't here."

"I'm sure she can live without it," muttered Suzie.

"But it's important to know what's going on. It keeps you alert. Otherwise there's a danger you might start getting careless and running risks."

"Not much chance of Jean-Guy letting her do that," said someone.

"Honestly," said someone else, "he's like a mother hen!"

"I think it's rather sweet," said Suzie.

"Oh, well, of *course*," huffed Marcia, "if one's content to play the little woman and have a *man* for protection –"

"I wouldn't mind!" said Carmen.

"Me, neither!" Suzie twisted round to check the seam of her tights. "Specially if it was Jean-Guy…"

The subject of the Butcher was mercifully let drop. Whatever morbid fascination his activities might once have held for me was fast disappearing. Never again, I vowed, would I go and wallow in a film like *The Silence of the Lambs*. This was too close to home for comfort. Suddenly it wasn't just "unknown victims" but my own twin sister who might be lying there on a mortuary slab.

I don't know how I managed to get through that evening. For once, even the magic of *Les Sylphides* failed to cast its spell. Simple though it is (and deeply despised by Jean-Guy, who resents having to dance in the traditional black jerkin and white shirt with big floppy bow at the neck) I had always before been soothed by its ethereal beauty. No matter how tired, how cross, how stuffed full of cold or suffering from stomach cramps I may have been, *Sylphides* has had the power to transport me. Not that night. That night visions of Claire kept obtruding themselves between me and the moonlight. Hideous spectres which dispelled all magic.

Neither Jean-Guy nor I was wanted in the last ballet of the evening, Jean-Guy because it wasn't one of the ones in his repertoire, me because it used only six members of the corps and I wasn't amongst them, which meant that by nine o'clock we were free to leave the theatre.

We went for a meal to the same place we had gone to the previous night, with Tracey. It was rather dark and secretive (Jean-Guy likes not to be recognized: he says it becomes tiresome), with wonderful crimson banquettes that you could relax into instead of the usual hard seats, and every table enclosed in its own little alcove.

"Right. Now! Tell me." Jean-Guy leaned back on his banquette, one arm lazily stretched along the length of it. "What is all this nonsense about being worried?"

"You know I am!" I said.

"I know the neurotic Yank is; I didn't think you were quite so silly. Out of all the millions of people who inhabit this city, what makes you think this latest poor girl has to be Claire? Because that is what you're thinking, isn't it?"

"It said in the paper she might be English," I muttered.

"On what grounds?"

I hardly liked to say "Marks & Spencer underwear". It sounded too – well, flimsy, if you'll pardon the expression. After all, they *do* have a Marks in Paris; the French flock there. Some of them even think it's quite chic to bedeck themselves in St Michael.

I mumbled, "Her clothes looked English."

"Her clothes looked English. So you instantly jumped to the conclusion that it had to be Claire." Slowly, Jean-Guy shook his head. "What do I have to do to set your fears at rest? You want me to go to the police and check it out?"

"I –" I hesitated. For Jean-Guy to go to the police would lend credence to my fears. It would seem to confirm that there was indeed something to be concerned about.

"Listen." He leaned across the table towards me. "They want members of the public to come forward, right? So, OK! I'll come forward. Please, sir, may I go and see the stiff? Which won't be

Claire, I can tell you that here and now. But if it's going to stop you palpitating –" His hand closed over mine. "As soon as we've eaten I'll drop you off and turn myself in at the nearest cop shop. Assuming they don't instantly clap me behind bars, I shall then come back and report and we can both have a good night's sleep. How about that?"

I grinned, rather sheepishly. Jean-Guy was so matter-of-fact that he almost managed to convince me my fears were foolish and exaggerated. There was just that one little niggle of doubt that refused to go away.

"You can then, if you like, ring the neurotic Yank and put his mind at rest, as well."

"You don't care for him," I said, "do you?"

Jean-Guy shrugged; one of his totally over-the-top, shoulders-up-to-the-ears jobs.

"I guess he's all right – for Claire. He wouldn't do for you."

"Why not?"

"You'd be bored to death in no time."

"He told me something yesterday," I said. "I meant to tell you, but I forgot. This guy that was pestering Claire … he said he'd asked Mme Dastugue if she had any idea who he might be and she said there'd been someone that used to call round and that he was – was tall and dark and – had the key."

"So he must have been someone Claire trusted.

She wouldn't give the key to just anyone. I'll bet that's solved your mystery! She's run off with the tall dark handsome stranger."

I objected. "No one said he was handsome! And in any case, she's not very likely to have run off with someone she didn't want to be alone with."

Not very likely to have run off with anyone.

"You've only got the Yank's word she didn't want to be alone with him."

"So why should he make it up?"

Another shrug. "Finish off your coffee and let me go and get this other business over."

"I hope it doesn't get into the papers." I was beginning to have cold feet now that the moment of truth had arrived. DANCER GOES TO VIEW BODY. I could just see it in the headlines.

"Why should it get into the papers?"

"Well, if someone were to recognize you."

"No one is going to recognize me."

"But you'll have to tell them your name!"

Jean-Guy gave me a pitying look. "Do you honestly think your average copper has ever even heard of Vaslav Nijinsky, let alone Jean-Guy Fontenille? I'm a dancer, not a pop star!"

It was true, the average person in the street wouldn't look twice at him – or at least, they would, but not because they knew who he was. The only time Jean-Guy was bothered by people wanting autographs, apart from at the stage door after a performance, was when he went to dine in smart restaurants near the theatre.

We took a cab back to Neuilly but instead of having him drop me at the flat I begged to be allowed to stay in his room in the hotel and wait for him there.

"Or I could – come with you, if you like."

"No need. I can handle it."

I am such a coward: I let him go on his own.

Time never passed so slowly as while I was waiting for Jean-Guy to come back. One look at his face, when he finally came through the door, and I knew the worst.

"*Claire?*"

I had never fainted in my life before. When I came to, I found myself sitting on the edge of the bed with Jean-Guy pushing my head between my knees.

"Vicky!" He gave me a little slap on the cheek. "Vicky, it's all right! Ça va, ça va!"

I looked at him, with glazed eyes. What did he mean, ça va?

"It wasn't Claire!"

"It – wasn't – Claire?"

"No!" He took a miniature brandy from the bar. "Here!" He wrenched off the top and poured the contents into a glass. "Drink!"

I did so, obediently, the merest sip, and nearly choked. Jean-Guy stroked my hair away from my face.

"What made you jump to that ridiculous conclusion?"

How could I tell him that as he had walked through that door he had looked like someone who has gazed upon the ultimate horror?

"Was it – really – not Claire?" I whispered.

"Really and truly … it was not Claire."

"I'm sorry. I'm sorry!" I felt foolish now – and guilty, too. "I should never have asked you to go!"

"You didn't ask me, I offered."

"And you are – you are quite certain?"

"Vicky, *crois-moi!* I am absolutely positive." He raised the glass to his own lips and emptied it in one gulp. "Please don't ask me anything more. It's an experience I really would rather try and forget."

"I'm sorry." I said it again, very humbly. And then, unable to stop myself, "I suppose they wanted to know who you were and why you'd gone there?"

"Oh, yes." He nodded, grimly. "Name, address, fingerprints … I got the full works. I had the impression that for two pins they'd have locked me in a cell and held me for questioning."

I stared at him, appalled. "You don't think they seriously thought you had anything to do with it?"

"Oh, probably not." Jean-Guy was starting to sound weary. "It just felt that way. *Viens!*" He held out a hand. "Let's get you back to the flat."

I wondered, as we walked along the rue Fleury, whether Jean-Guy would be going off as usual to sit in a bistro — perhaps even to get a little bit drunk and wipe out the memory of what he'd been through — but I didn't like to ask in case he thought I was prying or even attempting to tag along.

We reached the entrance to the flats.

"You don't need to come all the way up," I said. "Honestly!"

He insisted, however.

"I'll just see you safely locked away."

It was as well that he did, for as I opened Claire's door a dark shape sprang out at me.

7

"Claire!"

I found myself snatched at, grabbed, almost shaken. I'm ashamed to admit that I reacted just as women always do when you see them in horror movies: I screamed. His grip on my shoulders tightened.

"Where have you been? I've—"

"Sorry, chum!" It was at that point that Jean–Guy intervened and wrenched him off me. "You've got the wrong person. This is Vicky, not Claire."

"Vicky?" He recoiled, dropping his hands immediately. He had some kind of accent, quite thick. I couldn't place it at first; I thought it might be Italian. "I beg your pardon! I am Fernando de Almeida. I am looking for Claire."

"We're all looking for Claire," said Jean-Guy. "Do you mind telling us what you're doing in the flat?"

"I have been telephoning – I have been calling. For three days I have been calling! In the end I am forced to use my key."

So this was the person to whom Claire had entrusted the right of coming and going – the guy who had been pestering her, whom she no longer wanted to be alone with. The tall, dark, and – yes, handsome, stranger. I wouldn't have trusted him. I thought he looked creepy. His eyes were too deep set, his nose too thin, with those funny fly-away nostrils, and his hair, as black as Jean-Guy's but dead straight rather than wavy, slicked back from a widow's peak, gleaming and glistening as if it had had oil rubbed into it.

He was undeniably handsome – almost too much so for my taste. I find I distrust people who are too good-looking, both men and women. Jean-Guy is beautiful, but you can look at Jean-Guy and imagine him stripped to the waist digging holes in the road or shifting tons of horse manure; you couldn't imagine Fernando like that. I realize it probably helps that I have personally seen Jean-Guy when he is definitely not at his best. In morning class, for example, unshaven with a sweat band round his head, dressed in the usual ragbag assortment of T-shirt, tights, leg warmers, etc., that passes for practice clothes with dancers, bathed in perspiration, sweating and grunting at the barre with the rest of us, which I suppose does take some of the shine off. But honestly, you could never in a month of Sundays have pictured Fernando getting himself in a lather.

"Have you known Claire long?" I said.

"Since eight months." He looked at me, rather wildly. "We are engaged to be married and th—"

"*Married?*" I said. That I could not believe! Surely even Claire wouldn't get herself engaged to be married and fail to mention it to Mum and Dad? To me, perhaps; but not to her own parents. Claire has always been dutiful. But come to that, Claire wouldn't get herself engaged to be married full stop – and certainly not to someone as flash as Fernando. He wasn't her type at all. No wonder she'd complained to Tracey that he had been pestering her.

It was all most extraordinary, I thought. Claire had never, to my knowledge, had a boyfriend in her life, and now here they were coming out of the woodwork in all directions. I couldn't help wondering how many more were likely to turn up. What kind of secret life had my twin been leading?

I heard Jean-Guy, in level tones, suggest that we all repair to the nearest bistro to "talk things over".

"Since we seem to have something in common … we're all deeply interested in Claire's whereabouts."

Fernando was another who was not only

interested but also, or so he claimed, desperately worried. What Fernando was worried about was that she might have "done something silly".

"Such as what?" Jean-Guy sounded puzzled, as well he might. The thought of Claire doing anything silly was really quite novel.

"I worry —" Fernando announced it with deep intensity, his voice throbbing — "that she might have taken her life."

That jolted me.

"Why should she do that?" I said sharply.

"It is all my fault!" He groaned. "I should never have pushed her as I did."

"Pushed her?" I said. Absurdly, I had visions of Beachy Head. "Pushed her how?"

"As I say, we are engaged to be married. We are d—"

"Since when?"

"Since one month ago."

"Claire never said anything about it!"

He explained that the plan had been to wait until her birthday – *our* birthday – which was in August and then to make an official announcement to both sets of parents, ours in Cricklewood and his in Rio. (For the moment, my geography being what it is, I couldn't remember whether Rio de Janeiro was in Brazil or Argentina, but at any rate I knew it wasn't Italy.) They had then, it seemed, had this fantastic quarrel about how to bring the children up, whether as Roman Catholics or C. of E. Fernando had insisted they must be brought up as Catholics; Claire had insisted on C. of E. "until they were old enough to choose".

I thought, I can't believe I'm hearing this! Claire, getting engaged? Claire, discussing children? *Claire*, falling out over religion? We've never been a family for going to church. The last time Claire had set foot in one, as far as I was aware, was at our gran's funeral, three years ago. She certainly couldn't describe herself as C. of E. The school we went to was Methodist, if anything; at any rate they always held their carol service in the local Methodist church.

I gazed across the table at Fernando, agitatedly waving his hands – smooth and elegant, with supple fingers – as he expounded his fears of Claire having "done something silly". Was he the sort to weep and wail, or was he the sort to turn violent? In other words, had he merely embarrassed and irritated her, or had he actually terrified her? From what Tracey had said, I was willing to bet on the latter. It would certainly account for her having packed her bags and left in such an uncharacteristic rush. But she might at least have spared a thought for me, alone in the flat with Fernando still prowling the streets with the key in his pocket!

Another thought occurred to me: could it have been Fernando who had climbed on to the balcony that first night? Assuming that Claire had been in the flat, knowing that she would have the chain on the door and almost certainly wouldn't let him in, had he determined to get in anyway? To get in and – do what?

I felt a nasty slithering sensation down my spine, as if something chill and damp were wriggling its way through my vertebrae.

"Where did you meet Claire?" I said. My voice cut rather more loudly than I had intended across the stream of his melodramatic fancies. One thing I felt quite confident about: Claire would never "do anything silly".

He turned his deep-set gaze upon me and said that he and Claire had met in class – they were students at the same language school. He indicated that it had been a case of love at first sight. On his side, perhaps; I reckoned it would have taken a bit longer to kindle any flames in Claire. Maybe that was what had attracted him – what Jean-Guy always called her "Strictly not for touching" look.

Jean-Guy, of course, is a very physical person, so for him I could see that it would be a real turn-off – well, except that he wouldn't be interested in the first place, according to Marcia. Unless what she had told me was a gross exaggeration, which let's face it, it could have been. I mean, lots of people aren't absolutely exclusive in their proclivities, if that's the word. I could always dream…

Fernando, on the other hand, probably *was* exclusive – exclusively macho: red-blooded male. Yeeuch! Not my type at all. I like at least a bit of sensitivity. It's possible he'd never have met anyone like Claire before, demure and English and seemingly immune to his devastating charms. I wondered how long it would have taken him to win her over, and how long it would have taken her to come to her senses. Poor old Claire! I could imagine her panic when she finally realized what kind of guy she'd got mixed up with. That, I thought, was what came of holding yourself aloof all those years. I wouldn't have made that mistake.

"So when did you have this row?" I said.

He said stiffly that they had had the row – the quarrel – the disagreement – about a fortnight before term ended. It had led to Claire breaking off their engagement and throwing the ring back at him. (He claimed they'd bought one, though significantly he didn't produce it. You'd have thought he'd have hung on to it if he'd been all that cut up, which he assured us over and over that he was.)

"I am begging with her – pleading with her – please to change her mind. Every day, begging!"

I could see why she'd told Tracey he was pestering her. He wasn't simply intense, he was ... emotionally threatening. Those deep dark eyes bored into you so that you felt almost as if you were being skewered, being pinned into place on a specimen board. I shivered. Sooner Claire than me!

In the end, he told us, shamefaced, he had "lost all my patience" (*His* patience? What about Claire's?) and had left her to get on with it.

"So you haven't seen her since – since when?" said Jean-Guy.

Since the language school broke up for the Easter vacation, he told us. On a sudden impulse he'd booked himself on a flight and gone back to Brazil, intending to wipe Claire from his mind. It wasn't good for him, he said, it wasn't good for his studies, to be perpetually tormented. But then once back in Brazil he couldn't stop thinking of her, he'd even tried telephoning her several times and had grown worried when there was never any reply, which was what had brought him back to Paris, three days ago, since when he'd gone on telephoning and had finally, in despair, called round and let himself in with his key.

"You could have asked Mme Dastugue," I said. "She'd have told you Claire wasn't there."

Fernando said that was what he had been about to do when we showed up. He said he normally tried to avoid Mme Dastugue because "she doesn't like me to have the key."

I didn't like him having the key, either. I waited for Jean-Guy to say forcefully that it would be better if he handed it back, but it didn't seem to occur to him so I said it myself. Fernando seemed surprised – even hurt.

"You want me not to have it?"

"I'd have thought," I said, "when she broke off the engagement she'd have asked for it back anyway."

"She didn't. It was the one thing that gave me hope."

My betting was she had, and he'd refused. I'd have called the police if I'd been her. Claire had absolutely no idea how to handle men.

"I guess it would be more sensible if we hung on to it." Jean-Guy said it almost apologetically. I glared at him. Why be apologetic to this creep? "Claire can always let you have it again when she comes back."

Claire wasn't that stupid, I thought. Sullenly, Fernando removed the key from a fancy key-ring (solid silver, it looked like. Solid silver, for a key-ring?) and handed it to Jean-Guy, who slipped it into his pocket. He didn't say anything, Fernando, but I felt the slithers down my spine again as his deep-sunk eyes bored into me. I thought, it wouldn't surprise me if he's already had another one cut...

Urgently, as Fernando went back inside (we were sitting out on the pavement) to buy another round of drinks, I said, "Do you think we ought to have the lock changed?"

"What for? You've got the key back."

I muttered about him having had another one cut, but Jean-Guy told me crisply not to be stupid.

"*Sois pas bête!*"

"I don't trust him," I whined. "All that junk about having kids and how to bring them up!"

"Very important," said Jean-Guy.

What would he know about it?

"Claire doesn't give tuppence for religion!"

"That doesn't mean to say she'd necessarily want her kids brought up as Catholics."

I was tempted to say, "Why not? You were." But that would have been flippant and in any case irrelevant.

"The point is," I said, "that this is all Alice in Wonderland. Claire wouldn't ever get engaged to a nerd like that! She wouldn't get engaged *period*."

"Why not? People do."

"Not at seventeen! Not Claire!"

"Well, she obviously did."

"It's not obvious at all!" I retorted, but Jean-Guy only went into another of his shoulder-hunching routines. I knew what he was thinking: she's already sent me off on a wild-goose chase to look at a dead body; what more does she want?

"People," I said, "do not act out of character just because they've come to Paris." Paris wasn't as special as all that. "Claire's about as likely to get engaged to some South American playboy as she is to become a – a belly dancer!" Which was just about the most unlikely thing I could think of on the spur of the moment.

Jean-Guy hunched his shoulders yet again – but just a mini shrug this time, indicating that as far as he was concerned he was bored with the whole subject – and made no comment.

On the chair next to mine, Fernando had left his bag. (He carried one of those dinky little male shoulder-bags, wouldn't you know it?) It was open, and from one corner the edge of his passport protruded. With an eye on the door of the bistro, I whipped it out and began flicking through it.

"Vicky! What are you doing?" Jean-Guy hissed it at me. I think he was actually quite shocked.

"Look." I held it open. "It's hardly been used. Austria last year. Mexico. France – September. That's when he came here. He hasn't been out of the country since then. I thought he was supposed to have gone back to Brazil?"

Jean-Guy was still trying to think of some likely explanation when Fernando himself returned.

"Sorry," I said, holding the passport out to him. "I knocked your bag and it fell out. But I couldn't help noticing ... it doesn't seem to have any stamp for when you went to Brazil."

It broke him immediately. I honestly hadn't expected it to. I'd expected him to try bluffing, to say they'd forgotten, or they hadn't bothered, or he'd used a temporary passport. Instead, mumbling slightly, he admitted that he hadn't gone back to Brazil, he'd stayed in France.

"In Paris?" I said.

He shook his head, cradled in his hands. Not in Paris. He'd been in the Loire Valley with another student from the language school. An American girl student. Not a particular friend of Claire's, but obviously someone who was known to her. Now he felt terrible about it. He felt he'd betrayed her, even though it was she who'd broken off the engagement. That was why he'd lied to us, because he hadn't wanted it to get back to Claire.

A likely tale, I thought.

He raised his head and gave me one of his penetrating stares.

"Do you believe me?"

"Why shouldn't we?" said Jean-Guy.

"I don't know, but she doesn't!"

No, I didn't. I was beginning to have horrible feelings inside me. I was beginning to wonder whether in fact it was Claire who had gone with him to the Loire Valley – suddenly, foolishly, on a whim. Had gone with him, but not come back...

"You want proof? I give you proof! Here –" Fernando pulled a napkin towards him and began stabbing at it, furiously, with his pen. (Gold, naturally. Eighteen carat, I daresay.) He pushed the napkin towards me. "You don't believe me, you go and ask!"

"For crying out loud!" Jean-Guy snatched up the napkin and tried to thrust it back at Fernando but wasn't quite quick enough: I got there first.

"Oh, now, come on! This is ridiculous," he said. "We're not here to check up on people."

"Ask her!" said Fernando. "Tell her I told you!"

"We shall do no such thing," said Jean-Guy, when Fernando had angrily taken his departure and we were walking back up the rue Fleury for the second time that night.

"Why not?" I challenged him. "I'd like to know if his story's true."

He stopped, exasperated. "Why in God's name shouldn't it be?"

"I don't know." I pursed my lips. "It's just a feeling I have."

"Yes, like the feeling you had that it was going to be Claire they pulled out of that ice box!"

"Look, I already said I'm sorry about that! I'm sorry, I'm sorry! I should have been the one to go. It obviously upset you —"

"Dead right it upset me! Just don't go upsetting me any more! She writes a note, she says she'll see you soon — what else do you want?"

I wanted proof that at least some part of Fernando's story was true.

I pulled the crumpled napkin from my pocket and straightened it out.

"Grace Arnold, 4/24 rue des Soeurs, Paris XV."

No telephone number; that was a pity. I'd like to have spoken to her there and then (before Fernando could get at her). "Where is rue des Soeurs?"

"How should I know?" Jean-Guy said it roughly.

"I thought you were supposed to know Paris inside out?"

"I don't know every shabby, sordid, squalid little back street."

"Who says it's a shabby, sordid, squalid little back street?"

"It has to be, if I don't know it."

"Well, anyway," I said, "I can find out."

I'd been indoors about five minutes when the telephone rang. I thought it was probably Jean-Guy, ringing to apologize for being churlish. Maybe even ringing to say he'd had a change of heart and we'd go round to rue des Soeurs, to speak to Grace Arnold, as soon as we could get away from the theatre tomorrow. Even that he'd decided to spike Fernando's guns and go round there immediately, except that of course you couldn't really go calling on people at two o'clock in the morning if they didn't know you.

Anyway, it wasn't Jean-Guy, it was Tracey, calling from his computer room and seemingly unaware of the time. He was anxious to discover if I'd had any news. I filled him in, briefly, on all that had occurred. I could hear him sucking in his breath at the other end of the telephone when I told him about Fernando claiming to have been engaged to Claire.

"She never mentioned anything about that to me!"

"Nor me," I said. "Not that she would, necessarily, but it does seem a bit strange. You don't happen to know where the rue des Soeurs is, do you?"

"Rue des Soeurs? Sure!"

"You do?" I said.

"Sure I do! Why?"

I explained about Grace Arnold, and Fernando's story of having gone off to the Loire Valley with her.

"I wanted to go and check it out ... it's just a feeling I have. But Jean-Guy won't come with me."

"I'll come with you," said Tracey. "When do you want to go?"

I said that if I had my way I'd go right now, only perhaps if we did she wouldn't open the door to us. Tracey said, "We could give it a go if you really feel it's that important." But of course I didn't. I said, "No. Tomorrow will do."

If I'd taken him up on his offer, then who knows? We might have gone round to the rue des Soeurs right there and then, and everything might have turned out quite differently. Grace Arnold, poor girl, might still have been alive. As it was, we arranged for Tracey to meet me outside the stage door at four o'clock the next day; and by then, Grace Arnold was dead.

8

I slept much better that night, knowing that it was Jean-Guy who had the spare key rather than Fernando. I'd looked long and hard at the chain and it seemed to me that a really determined man could quite easily put his shoulder to the door and break it open.

Last night I'd actually gone to the trouble of lugging a heavy chest of drawers across the room as an added precaution. It still hadn't stopped me having nightmares.

This time I slept peacefully right through till morning, when the alarm clock shrilled and I crawled out of bed and prepared to go down the road to meet Jean-Guy at the Hotel Fleury, which was where we always had breakfast.

Over croissants and coffee we talked companionably of nothing in particular – I was speculating, I seem to recall, on whether I might share a flat with Suzie when we returned to London, rather than carry on living in Cricklewood and having to commute, which was a drag after an evening performance.

I didn't say anything about Tracey and his telephone call, nor what we had planned on doing at four o'clock. I'm not sure why I didn't mention it, except that Jean-Guy had made it quite plain, last night, that for whatever reason he didn't sanction my going round to the rue des Soeurs. Maybe I had just tried his patience too far; I don't know. But anyway I didn't mention it. Not that it would have made any difference at that stage, because by then Grace was already dead.

We travelled in to morning class together (in a cab: Jean-Guy won't use the Métro) just the same as usual. I had absolutely no premonitions of any kind whatsoever. There were no more lurid headlines in the papers and I had almost, even, stopped worrying about Claire. I wanted to check Fernando's story, but that was more because I instinctively didn't believe it than because I seriously thought he might have done something nasty.

In my own mind I felt pretty certain that Claire, being unused to entanglements with men, had run off in a panic when things became too hot for her to handle, and that Fernando might have gone off in a fit of pique with Grace Arnold or he might have stayed in Paris and sulked – or even brooded revenge, which was why he was so anxious to find her. I didn't honestly believe that he might have killed her. I don't think at that stage I believed he might have killed anybody. When Jean-Guy had returned from the police station with the news that whoever the unfortunate girl on the mortuary slab was, she wasn't Claire, I had determined to put all hysterical thoughts of the Butcher out of my head. That way lay madness, and I had a career to pursue.

Tonight we were doing the white act from *Swan Lake* and I was to dance a Little Swan. True, a Little Swan is hardly what you would call a solo role, let alone a vehicle for stardom, but there were only four of us so I reckoned it had to be a step up from merely being one of a flock. It was the first hint of promotion I had had and I was determined to make the most of it.

The day pursued its accustomed course – class, rehearsal, short break for lunch, run-through of Act II, and then I was free until the evening performance.

"Are you going out?" said Suzie.

"Yes; why? Did you want something?"

"Only a breath of fresh air. Is it OK if I come with you, or –"

She hesitated, obviously trying to be diplomatic. Or are you going with Jean-Guy was what she wanted to say.

They couldn't quite work out my relationship with Jean-Guy, but that wasn't surprising as I couldn't, either.

"I mean, just tell me," said Suzie, "if I'm going to be in the way."

I didn't feel like launching into lengthy explanations, especially if there were any danger of it getting back to Jean-Guy. I had a feeling he wouldn't be too pleased at the thought of my going off with Tracey. In spite of being Claire's boyfriend, he still, in Jean-Guy's book, counted as a stranger. So I just mumbled something about "meeting someone" and dashed off before she could ask questions.

Tracey was waiting for me as arranged, at the stage door.

"So how do we get to this place?" I said.

"Rue des Soeurs? Easy. Take the Métro. It's on a direct line."

I love the Métro; I love the names of the stations. Boissière, Trocadéro, Champ de Mars, Bir Hakeim, La Motte Picquet... (I have to suppose that Dollis Hill and Neasden sound just as fascinating to foreigners.)

We got out at La Motte Picquet, turned right along the Boulevard de Grenelle towards the Place de Cambronne, then left and right and left again into the rue des Soeurs. It wasn't exactly sordid or squalid but it was certainly shabby – and certainly a back street. Short, very narrow, and tucked away, with miscellaneous shops on either side.

Number 24 was half-way down. It was a sort of grocer's, or *épicerie*, or maybe delicatessen is the right word, selling exotic-looking cheeses and lengths of sausage. The entrance to the apartment rented by Grace Arnold was through a side door, and standing on the pavement outside were a couple of uniformed police, one speaking into a walkie-talkie.

"*Les flics*," said Tracey. "Wonder what they're doing there?"

We were very soon to discover. As we approached the door, they moved together to bar our way. The one that wasn't using the walkie-talkie said something which I couldn't catch, but which Tracey fortunately did. He must have asked who we wanted because Tracey said, "*Nous voulons voir quelqu'un qui habite ici. Elle s'appelle –*" he turned to me for confirmation – "Grace Arnold?"

I nodded. Tracey spoke fairly horrible French in a strong transatlantic accent, but he spoke it slowly, so that I could follow it. The flic said, "*Attendez*," (I think) and disappeared through the door.

"*Qu'est-ce qu'il y a?*" said Tracey, but the flic with the walkie-talkie simply shook his head and repeated, "*Attendez.*"

The other one then reappeared with a man in a suit, whom I guessed from his manner – very self-important and slightly hectoring – must be a plain-clothes detective. When he realized I couldn't speak much French he addressed us in English. He wanted to know who we were, how well we knew Grace, whether she had been expecting us, when we'd last seen her. I said that she hadn't been expecting us and that I'd never actually met her, but she was a student at the same language school as my sister. I added that Tracey had simply come along to show me the way, as he knew Paris and I didn't.

It was then that the plain-clothes man broke the news to us: Grace Arnold was dead, and he would be grateful if we would "accompany my colleague" to the police station to answer a few more questions.

We didn't really have much choice. I was too stunned by the news to say anything at all, beyond bleating rather piteously that I had to be back at the theatre in time for the evening performance, as if anyone cared for a thing like that. I assumed automatically that when he said Grace was dead, he meant that she had been murdered. It didn't seem feasible that a presumably healthy seventeen-year-old should suddenly drop dead from natural causes.

I allowed myself to be ushered into the back of a police car with Tracey. Tracey kept shaking his head and saying, "This is crazy, this is crazy," as if he couldn't believe what was happening – or what had happened. Not that anyone had told us any details at that stage. Those came later, in next morning's papers. For the moment all they were saying was that Grace was dead and that they wanted to ask us some questions.

At the police station we were taken to separate rooms. I was interviewed by another plain-clothes person, young and earnest with his hair shaved very short at the sides and standing up like the bristles of a brush in the centre. I kept staring at this hair and wanting to touch it to see if it were as spiky as it looked. A woman police person was put into the room with us, I suppose to stop me claiming that Bristle Brush had made a pass or improper advances.

"And so, Mlle!" He spoke excellent English did Bristle Brush. "What are you able to tell us?"

It all came pouring out of me. I practically gave him my life history. I explained about Claire being my twin and my coming to Paris to dance with the Barbican and how I was supposed to have been staying in Claire's flat with Claire, only Claire hadn't been there, and how she'd left me this note and how Fernando had been in the flat when I got back yesterday evening and how he'd claimed to have been engaged to Claire and said they'd had a row, and what the row was about, and how I just hadn't believed it, because of Claire not giving two straws about religion, and how Fernando had first said he'd gone off to Brazil and then changed his story and said he'd gone to the Loire Valley with this student from the language school, and I hadn't believed that, either, or at least I'd wanted to check up on it, and so Tracey had agreed to go with me to the rue des Soeurs because he knew where it was and I didn't.

And then I had to explain about Tracey, and how he had been Claire's boyfriend after she'd broken with Fernando, and how she was supposed to have had a date with him and she'd let him down, and how Tracey was worried because she'd told him some guy had been pestering her, and we were pretty sure that it must have been Fernando. And oh, yes, another thing. Fernando had had the key of the apartment, but now we had it back. And no, I didn't know where Fernando lived, but he was also a student at the language school. And no, come to that, I didn't even know which language school it was. Obviously I must have been told, but the name hadn't stuck. It might have been the Alliance Française, but I really wasn't sure. On the other hand, Tracey would probably know. And yes, I thought Claire might have mentioned Grace in one of her letters home, but I couldn't be absolutely sure about that, either, except I seemed to remember our mum saying that Claire had talked about an American girl; but then, of course, there might be lots of American girls.

All this was laboriously written down, and then taken away to be typed out so that I could read it through and sign it. While it was being typed I was given a cup of coffee, and it was then that they decided to ask me whether I'd been on my own with Fernando when we'd had the conversation about him going off to the Loire Valley with Grace Arnold or whether anyone had been with me who might be able to corroborate my story and/or give them any more information.

I was sorely tempted to tell them that I'd been on my own, but I knew of course that I couldn't. They were bound to find out and then it would be perjury or something and I'd be in trouble.

Reluctantly, I gave them Jean-Guy's name. As he had predicted, they hadn't the faintest idea who he was, but their computer must have been bang up to date because Bristle Brush went away and came back only minutes later to ask was that the same Jean-Guy Fontenille who had asked to look at a body and check that it was not Claire? (It wasn't until later that I realized this must mean they were linking Grace Arnold's murder – by now it had been more or less admitted that she had been murdered – to all the others that had taken place. Did they really think the Butcher had been responsible or did they always run everything through the computer on the off chance of finding connections?)

I was horrified when Bristle Brush informed me

that he had sent someone to the theatre to pick up Jean-Guy and bring him in for questioning.

"You may if you wish await him and we will take you back together."

I bleated again about the evening performance and was assured that "You will be there in time." In fact, as it happened, neither of us was wanted until the second half, for Act II of *Swan Lake*, but Jean-Guy was still going to be furious. I couldn't say that I blamed him. He was a Company star; Company stars have to guard their reputations. It wasn't going to do him much good, being publicly dragged off to a police station.

I didn't see Jean-Guy until they had finished with him and brought him out to the room where Tracey and I sat waiting. Tracey, very sweetly, had offered to stay and keep me company; I was glad enough of it. Police stations are pretty inhospitable places even when you are simply there as an innocent member of the public "helping with inquiries". Also, by now, I was not only worried about Jean-Guy but had started once again to worry about Claire. Bristle Brush had listened intently to my story and taken all the details, and although he'd assured me that she would "almost certainly" turn up alive and well in her own good time, he hadn't dismissed my fears out of hand as being groundless or hysterical. I had the feeling that Claire's name was going to be added to the computer, alongside all the details of the victims who had already been discovered. Why else would he have asked me to let him know "the minute she comes back"?

Jean-Guy appeared looking grim. He nodded curtly to Tracey and took my arm as if to say "Let's get the hell out of here". I don't think he was best pleased when Tracey climbed into the police car with us, but he deserved a lift just as much as we did and anyhow it was on our way.

"I'll call you," he said, as we dropped him outside his apartment block.

One of Jean-Guy's eyebrows curved in an irritable arc. "What does he want to call you for?"

"Just for news of Claire?" I said. I said it pleadingly, in the hope I might get away without being lectured at. Jean-Guy just humped a shoulder and went "Hmph!"

He was, I had to say it, really quite restrained; not only while we were in the car, with the police driver able to hear what we were saying, but even afterwards, over dinner in what had become our usual spot. He let me babble on about how Tracey had rung me and how I had told him about Fernando and how I had asked him if he knew where the rue des Soeurs was, and how he had said yes, "And I didn't want to put you to any trouble so I thought if I went round there with him we could speak to her and just check the story out and *of course* I would have told you afterwards —"

"Of course," said Jean-Guy.

"Well, I would!"

"A pity you couldn't have told me before. Maybe we could have avoided all the upset."

I said soberly, "The only way we could have avoided it was if we'd gone round last night."

"Meaning what?"

"Meaning she – she might still have been alive."

"Oh?" The eyebrow went curving again. "How do you know that?"

"Well –" I stopped. I didn't, did I? Last night might have been too late: Grace might already have been dead. No one had said when she was actually killed. No one had said *how* she was killed. The police, in fact, had given away very little.

"We couldn't possibly have gone round there last night. You know that as well as I do. And even if we had, what difference would it have made? We'd simply be even more suspect than we are now."

"*Suspect?*" I said. I gaped at him. "They can't think *we* did it!"

"Not you," he agreed. "But you can bet your life I'm on their books."

I thought wretchedly that Jean-Guy would rue the day he had promised to keep an eye on me. I also wondered what I was going to say to Mum next time I rang her, which would have to be soon; she would panic if she didn't receive regular bulletins. Even with Claire – sensible Claire, who could be trusted – she insisted on fortnightly telephone calls. I couldn't decide whether it was a good thing or a bad thing that the last call had occurred just a few days before we left for Paris. Mum had told me, all cosily, that "Claire rang. She's really excited at having you over there."

Mum had been so happy that Claire and I were becoming good friends at last.

The next call wouldn't be due for another week. I decided that on the whole it had to be a good thing since it meant that whatever the outcome Mum could at least enjoy a few more worry-free days. There was no point in getting her in a tizz before it was necessary. I further decided that *I* wouldn't get in a tizz until that week had come and gone. If Claire hadn't rung home by then, I would know there was cause for concern.

The next day, the news had broken and was in all the papers, with the usual screeching headlines in *France Soir*.

ANOTHER PIECE OF BUTCHERY?

The question mark was there not because the murder of Grace Arnold hadn't been brutal, but because the police couldn't be sure whether it was the work of the Butcher or whether there was a second maniac stalking the streets of Paris. The killing bore "certain resemblances" to the method employed by the Butcher. The only difference was that poor Grace had met her end in her own flat rather than in the Bois de Boulogne, which was where all the other murders had taken place – or at least where all the other bodies had been found.

"*Police say that in all other respects it bears the hall-marks of the Butcher. They have revealed for the first time a detail pr*—" Marcia stopped.

"What?" said someone.

"*A detail previously* –" she swallowed – "*previously suppressed. In all cases, including this l*—"

I clamped my hands to my ears. I didn't want to know what the police had previously suppressed. If it were lurid enough to halt even Marcia in her tracks, it would certainly turn the stomachs of more sensitive mortals such as myself. I didn't want to hear!

But I did; unfortunately. And I knew that I was going to have nightmares.

There was a stunned silence as Marcia finished reading. Then Carmen, in a small voice, said: "How did they manage to identify the body if – if the head –" She stopped.

"It was her flatmate." Marcia sounded more subdued than I had ever heard her. "Her flatmate came in and – discovered the body."

"But how did she know that it was her?"

"It – had to be. I suppose. The – clothes or – something."

I made an effort: there was a question that had to be asked. "Does it say – when – she was killed?"

Marcia shook her head. The nearest they had got to pinpointing the time of the murder was "Somewhere in the early hours of the morning."

I thought, Fernando could have gone straight round there…

"She must have known the guy?" Josie said it pleadingly. No one could bear the thought that it might have been quite random. "She surely must have known him or she wouldn't have let him in?"

"Unless he got in through the window while she was asleep… It says here –" Marcia referred back to the paper – "it says one of the windows was closed but not locked, so they think whoever did it must have got out that way and gone across the roof. But for all they know, he could have got *in* that way. Maybe."

A slight involuntary shudder ran through me. I was remembering that first night, and the shadow of a man on the balcony. Jean-Guy had tried his best to persuade me it was a cat, but I had never really been convinced.

"I always sleep with all the windows closed even if it is like a sweat box," said Josie.

"What, even in the hotel? We're on the third floor!"

"Yes, but there's a flat roof outside my room."

"If I were you," said Carmen, "I'd ask for another one."

"I think I will. This is horrible!"

113

Horrible was an understatement. Try as I might, I couldn't wipe my mind clear of the sickening details read out by Marcia. There was something about them which bothered me, over and above the sheer hideous brutality of it all.

"How did they manage to identify the body?" Carmen had asked.

It nagged at me. Something, somewhere, wasn't right; but I couldn't at that moment put my finger on what it was. That was to come later...

We danced the same programme that night as we had on opening night, with Jean-Guy as Albrecht. He was concerned because some special do had been laid on for himself and the other principals (not for minor soloists and certainly not for members of the corps, though we do get to go to parties sometimes) and he didn't want me making my own way home.

I am not usually any more of a wimp than the next person, but I have to admit I wasn't too keen on the idea myself; not after hearing what had happened to poor Grace Arnold. I tried to be brave. I said, "Look, I can always get a cab."

Jean-Guy wouldn't hear of it. He insisted on seeing me safely back to the flat – and not just to the main entrance, but all the way up the stairs. He even waited while I put my key in the lock and switched the light on.

"I don't want to take any chances," he said.

It was strange that he had never been in the least bit worried about Claire going off, he had never really accepted that there was any cause for alarm, yet here he was fussing over me with as much attention to detail as even Mum would have approved of. He checked the windows were properly closed, he checked I had removed the key from the front door, he even – yes! He even cast his eye over the tiny bathroom, just in case someone might be lurking there.

"OK! Now you keep that chain on the door," he said, "and don't open for anyone. And that means *anyone*. Right?"

"Right." I nodded. "Enjoy the party!"

He pulled a face. "This is strictly duty."

I was too wide awake for bed. The thoughts were still whizzing round my head, endlessly chasing their tails and getting nowhere. I felt the need to be occupied.

I hadn't had my usual post-performance meal, so I opened a can of soup and ate some cheese and an apple, then pottered for a while, sewing ribbons on to new pairs of point shoes, which was a job I should have done ages ago, then bashing at the blocks with a hammer which I found under the sink. You have to bash them or they make dreadful clopping noises on the stage, plus they cripple you. I know some people who actually break the backs by jamming them in doors. It seems hard on the shoe-makers who go to such lengths to fashion these dainty objects that we dainty dancers then promptly set about destroying them. They're like rags by the end of a ballet such as *Giselle*.

I knelt on the floor with my little hammer and happily battered and smashed until someone in the flat below took exception and started hammering angrily back on the ceiling, at which point I decided I'd better give up for the night and do something more socially acceptable, such as having a bath.

Once I get in a bath, I'm there for the duration – i.e., at least three changes of water, and washer-woman's fingers at the end of it. I was on my second change, attempting to operate the hot tap with my toes to save having to sit up, when I heard a sound that made me freeze: someone was knocking at the door...

9

My first thought was that it must be the angry neighbour from downstairs, come to complain about all the banging that had taken place. I pulled on my dressing-gown and pattered apprehensively barefoot across the parquet floor, desperately dredging up what little of my schoolgirl French I could remember.

Je m'excuse – excusez-moi – pardonnez –

I was about to open the door just the merest slit, keeping the chain on, when I belatedly remembered what I had promised Jean-Guy: don't open to *anyone*. Not even angry neighbours.

Feeling utterly foolish, I put my mouth to the crack and tried to speak through it.

"Allô?" I said, the way the French say it on the telephone.

"Vicky?"

I recoiled: it was Fernando. How had he managed to get in? (We discovered later, when the police were conducting their investigations, that he had conned a girl on the ground floor, which just goes to show that no system is ever foolproof.)

"*Vicky!*" He banged on the door with his fist.

Nervously I put my mouth back to the crack. "What is it? What do you want?"

"I have to speak with you! You told the police – you told them I murdered Grace!"

"I didn't!" I squeaked.

"Then why do they try to accuse me?"

"I d–don't know!"

I cast round desperately for something to jam against the door. Could I manage to drag the chest over there before he put his shoulder to it? I was sure the chain wouldn't hold.

"They say where is Claire!" He banged again, and this time rattled the handle.

"Well, where is she?" I yelled, lugging at the chest.

"This is what I have to talk to you about!" His tone suddenly changed; became honeyed, almost wheedling. "Let me in, Vicky! Please!"

"I'm sorry, I can't." Puffing and panting, I shoved the chest into place.

"Why not? What are you doing? Vicky, I am begging you!"

"I can't! I promised Jean-Guy!" Even now, when there was a possible mass murderer on the other side of the door, I felt this absurd need to be polite and rational. Pathetic, really; it must be something to do with one's upbringing.

"Just go away!" I begged. "Just go away and leave me alone!"

"Vicky, if you care at all about Claire –"

"I do care about her, but he made me promise! And anyway," I added, whimpering, "I've got to be up for class in the morning!"

He didn't say anything more after that. I heard him breathing, heavily, on the other side of the door, then I heard the creak of the stairs as he went back down. Or pretended to go back down. I turned, and sprang across to the telephone, my fingers fumbling as I punched out the number of Jean-Guy's hotel.

He wasn't there, of course; he must still be at the party. I left a message for him, saying that Fernando had been round, trying to get in, and I was scared he might come back again. Truth to tell, I was scared he might not really have gone. Suppose he did his old trick of coming across the roof and jumping down on to the balcony? The balcony doors were locked, but who would ever hear if he smashed the glass? I was isolated, all by myself at the top of the building. The nearest neighbour – the one I had annoyed – was two flights down.

Panic set in. I tore back to the telephone and

scrabbled in my bag for the numbers that Tracey had given me. My bag as usual looked as if mice had been making nests inside it: everything seemed to be shredded or crumpled or chewed.

I found what I was looking for under several layers of paper handkerchief. Home number, work number. I tried his work number first, but they said he hadn't come in. With unsteady fingers, keeping my ears cocked for the sounds of movement outside the door, my eyes locked into focus on the balcony, watching for the slightest hint of feet descending, I dialled his home number. Let him be there! Please God, let him be there!

"Hallo?" said Tracey. His soft Canadian drawl (he came from Ottawa, he'd told me) was comforting after Fernando's thick South American accent.

"Tracey? It's me," I said, "it's Vicky, I'm –"

"You heard from Claire?"

"No, but Fernando's been round. Just. He was mad at me for shopping him to the police. He wanted to come in only I wouldn't let him, s—"

"Dead right you don't let him! Where is he now?"

"I'm not sure. I think he went away, but—"

"I'll come around. Just hang on and don't move – and if he comes back, for God's sake don't open that door!"

"No," I said, "I won't." And then, in sudden terror, "Tracey, be careful! He might still be in the building."

"I can take care of myself," he said.

I hoped he was right. I had these visions of a maddened Fernando lurking in the darkened corridor with an axe in his hand.

I supposed if I'd had the least particle of sense I would have rung the police. I wondered afterwards why I hadn't but to be perfectly honest it never even occurred to me – maybe because I didn't know how. In England my fingers would have been scrabbling out 999 almost automatically, but how do you do it in a foreign country? Either Jean-Guy or Tracey seemed a much safer bet. Anything not to be left on my own with a possible mass murderer prowling the building.

Tracey must have called a cab, for barely five minutes after I'd rung him the intercom buzzed, almost frightening me into total paralysis. I flipped the switch and nervously said, "Hallo?"

"It's me," said Tracey. "You want to let me in?"

"Be careful!" I begged. "He might still be around."

I pressed the button that opened the main downstairs door and hovered apprehensively by the chest, with my ear to the crack, rigid with fear lest Fernando were skulking out there. He obviously wasn't, for within seconds Tracey had come bounding up the stairs and I was hastily hauling the chest of drawers back into position – embarrassed, now, by what I was beginning to think had been a hysterical over-reaction.

"I'm really sorry about this," I said. "I feel a bit

stupid ... I shouldn't have dragged you out at this time of night." Except by then it was morning – half-past midnight.

"You didn't drag me out," he said. "I chose to come."

"Well, yes, I know, but –"

"Please don't apologize." He shunted his glasses. "It suited me very well."

"It did?" I looked at him, doubtfully.

"Sure! I was wondering what to do for kicks."

"You weren't at work," I said.

"No; I didn't feel like it. I told them I had a migraine." He grinned at me; one of his mischievous, boy-next-door sort of grins. "I do that sometimes."

"Well, I'm afraid it's not going to be much fun round here. I haven't even got a drink I can offer you ... just a cup of coffee."

"A cup of coffee'll do fine." He dumped his jacket on a chair. "Where's Jean-Guy?"

I pulled a face. "At a party."

"How come you didn't get to go?"

"Wasn't invited; it's only for principals. I tried calling him before I got in a panic and called you, but he's not back yet."

"How about the cops? Did you call them?"

"No!" I turned, slowly, kettle in hand. That was the first time it struck me: maybe I should have done. "You think I should?"

"I guess it wouldn't hurt. You go ahead and make the coffee, I'll do it for you."

I listened as Tracey explained, in stumbling French, what had occurred.

"*Il est venu ici – il a frappé à la porte – il a crié comme un dément –*"

I wondered again if I had over-reacted. After all, the police had already interviewed Fernando and let him go, so they obviously didn't believe he was guilty of anything. I said as much to Tracey as I carried the coffee over.

"I hope they don't haul him in again. They've put him through it once."

I suddenly saw him not as a mass murderer, or any other kind of murderer, but as someone who was desperate.

"Vicky." Tracey sat down on the sofa beside me. He spoke seriously, earnestly. "A girl has been brutally done to death. Several girls have been brutally done to death. For all we know –" he paused, and shunted his spectacles. "For all we know, Claire has been brutally done to death."

I felt my cheeks drain of colour. It was the first time Tracey had ever actually admitted such a possibility.

"You don't – really think –"

He shook his head. "I don't know any more what to think. After what happened yesterday to that poor girl –"

"If we'd only gone round there straight away!"

"And then there was that one they never got to identify – that one recently –"

"That wasn't Claire." I said it quickly, relieved at least to be able to scotch that idea.

He looked at me. "How do you know?"

"Jean-Guy –" I stopped.

"Jean-Guy?" said Tracey.

"He – went to – look at the body."

Suddenly, I knew. I knew what it was that had been bothering me. If that sickening detail revealed by the police were true, how had Jean-Guy been able to identify the body as not being Claire? There was only one way I could think of, and that was her birthmark.

Did Jean-Guy know about Claire's birthmark?

Obviously he must do. (But *how*?)

He must do! He wouldn't have told me a lie. He wouldn't have said it wasn't Claire unless he were absolutely certain.

Little tendrils of doubt, all the same, had begun to creep in.

Tracey must have noticed a sudden drop in my confidence for he said gently, "Don't worry about Claire. I'm sure she's all right."

"But – you said – just a moment ago –"

"Forget what I said. Nothing has happened to Claire."

I wished I could be so certain. I wasn't even

certain, any longer, that Jean-Guy had told me the truth. I wasn't even certain, any longer, about Jean-Guy ... this was like a nightmare!

"Vicky?" Tracey was leaning in towards me. "What is it? What's the matter?"

"The sort of person – the sort of person –" I clutched both hands to my head. "What sort of person is it that can do these things?"

"Well, now, that's a big question. If anyone could answer that one –"

"They're mad," I said, "aren't they? They have to be mad!"

A little wriggle of a frown crossed his brow.

"Uh ... I wouldn't say mad, necessarily. Logical, according to their own lights. There's always a reason. Usually something way back in their child-hood."

I thought of Jean-Guy's childhood. It hadn't exactly been normal. Dragged the length and breadth of Europe with a trapeze artist for a father. One-parent family by the age of ten. But loads of kids came from one-parent families! I had to stop this. For my own sanity.

"There's a kind of principle at work here," said Tracey. He shunted his glasses. "You know the guy – ah – huh!" He seemed embarrassed. "You know he enjoys himself before he – uh – does what he feels compelled to do?"

"No." I had had enough of the gruesome details.

I didn't need any more.

"Yeah, well, he does," said Tracey. "And it seems to me – I've been working on this, I've been doing a whole lot of thinking – it seems to me the principle involved is quite simple: you can't have pleasure without pain."

Alarm bells set off a clamour in my head. Dear God! Where had I heard that phrase before?

"It's the old puritan ethic ... pleasure is sinful: you have to suffer for it."

You can't have pleasure without pain. Not in this business.

"For me, this is a familiar precept. It was drummed into me as a child. On the seventh day, you shall atone for your sins – and sins are always pleasurable, aren't they?"

I nodded, dumbly. Everything, slowly and hideously, with inescapable logic, was beginning to slot into place.

Claire's note that had disappeared before I could have another look at it and check that the handwriting had indeed been hers. Who knew my twin's handwriting well enough to forge it?

The mysterious ramblings late at night, the visits to Paris –

Claire's birthmark!

"He was pretty inventive, my dad." Tracey was still talking. "Sometimes he'd just take the strap to me, but other times, you know, he really worked at

126

it. The cupboard under the stairs, that was one of his favourites. He —"

"Cupboard under the s-stairs?" I said, striving to show an interest. The terrifying thoughts were still whirling and whizzing in my head.

"Yeah. It was like a little room ... dark and creepy. If I'd been really sinful – if I'd had a really good time, enjoying myself – like, say, it had been my birthday or Christmas, or something – well, then, I knew come Sunday I was going to have to pay for it. That cupboard sure did give me the heebie-jeebies."

I stared at him, horrified, suddenly alive to what he was saying. "You mean he shut you in there? In a *cupboard*?"

"Mm-hm." Tracey nodded. "I got so I was kind of used to it. I preferred it to some of the other stuff. At least I knew what I was getting into. Some of the other stuff was really – you know! Bizarre. He really got turned on by it. I can see that now. Of course at the time it seemed quite natural. This was my dad, for heaven's sake! Anything your dad does has to be right. Kids accept these things. It's only later you realize the damage that's been done. I don't need to go into analysis. I have myself pretty well sussed out."

"What about your mother?" I said. "She just let him?"

"I guess she got her kicks that way. They were a

pretty well-matched couple, my mum and dad. I'm only telling you all this junk so's you'll understand how it is I know about this particular principle I was talking about."

I looked at him, uncertainly. "What – principle?"

"You know!" He shunted his glasses. "No pleasure without pain."

"Oh! Yes."

I'd had to sleep on the sofa, I remembered. I'd woken up all full of aches, moaning that I had arthritis.

There's no pleasure without pain ... not in this business.

I shivered.

"Don't do that, Vicky!" Tracey stretched out a hand and stroked my hair. "I'm not going to hurt you."

"P-pardon?" I said.

"I don't like to hurt people. I'm not like my mum and dad. It upsets me to hurt people. It's just that – you know!" He said it regretfully. "Sometimes it's necessary."

"N–necessary?" I said.

"Like I told you ... you can't have one without the other."

"No!" I sprang to my feet and began, rather agitatedly, to pace the room. What was I going to say to the police when they came? What was I going to tell them?

"The worst thing is," said Tracey, "the really worst thing of all, the thing that really, really upsets me, is when they scream."

"What?" I came to a sudden stop. What was he talking about?

"I can't stand it when people scream. It gets the vibrations going in my head and then I don't enjoy myself." He smiled, and shunted his glasses. "I expect you think that's very peculiar."

"No, I – I don't think it's peculiar at all. I –"

"You what?"

"I –" I did another little turn about the room. "How long are these police going to take?"

"What police?"

"The cops?" I said. "The ones you called?"

"The ones I called?" He gave a sly grin; impish, amused. "I didn't call any cops, Vicky."

"Yes, you did! Just now! You said –"

"I know what I *said*."

"You mean –"

"Don't scream, Vicky!" He said it warningly, as he advanced across the room towards me. "I told you, I can't handle it when they scream."

"It was you!" I backed away from him, appalled. Too late, the realization hit me. "It was you, it was you!"

My voice rose to a shriek. Tracey was on me in an instant.

"I warned you, Vicky! I told you! I said, don't

scream! I can't take the noise!"

My heart began pounding, thumping hammer blows against my rib cage. Oh, Jean-Guy! I thought. Jean-Guy! You told me not to let anyone in!

"I'll ask you one more time." Tracey put a finger to my lips. "Please, Vicky ... don't scream."

My eyes slid sideways. The hammer I had used for bashing my ballet shoes was still lying on the floor. If I could just –

Just –

"No hammers, Vicky! I know you want to get at it. But how can I let you have a hammer?" His voice was soft and reproachful. "I can't let you have a hammer! You might hit me with it. Just relax!" He stroked his finger down my cheek. "Then we can have a good time together. OK?"

He smiled at me, his little-boy smile. Hopeful, companionable. I pressed myself back against the wall.

"What did you – do to Claire?" I whispered.

"Claire." His tone became wistful. "I didn't do anything to Claire. We never got that intimate. Would you believe –" he was leaning with his hands one on either side of me, supporting himself against the wall – "would you believe I was never in this place till that night I came through the windows and you took fright and ran away? I thought you were Claire. I'd hoped we were going to get to know each other. Properly. I really tried with that girl. But she was so cold. She is a really cold fish. Not like you, Vicky."

He stretched out a hand and gently, oh! so gently, ran his fingers through my hair. I did my best not to flinch.

"That's my girl! I like you much better than I liked her. You and me, we're going to have fun. I promise!"

"B–before we d–do," I croaked – I had this insane flicker of belief that if I could only keep him talking long enough something would happen – "why did you m–murder Grace Arnold?"

He frowned. "Please don't use that word. It's not at all a nice word to use."

"I'm sorry," I mumbled.

"Kindly rephrase your question."

"Why did you k–kill her?"

He grunted. "I'll accept that. I killed her. But what choice did I have? There's no pleasure without pain, Vicky. It always has to be paid for. You must surely understand?"

"I do understand." I assured him of it, earnestly. Anything to keep him happy. "But why Grace?"

"Oh! Well. I don't know, it seemed like a good idea. It was you put it into my head." He gave me a grin; conspiratorial, puckish. "Suggesting we go round and see her. I thought well, why not?"

"I c–can't think why she l–let you in."

"People do. It's amazing! Isn't it amazing?"

"It is if – if they don't – know you."

"Oh, she knew me." He nodded, complacently. "We'd talked. I met her over coffee, same as I met Claire ... same as I met most of them. She asked me back with her one time, only I wasn't in the mood right then. You have to be in the mood. You know what I mean? That night when I called you, part of the reason was that I was really feeling like it." He laughed, a little shamefacedly.

"I was actually fantasizing about you, if you want to know the truth. But still, Grace was nice. I enjoyed Grace. She had a warm personality. Unlike some I could name. Your sister, for example. Grace really wanted it. She was really screaming for it. But even she –" he shunted his spectacles – "even she had to go and ruin it in the end. I'm hoping you're going to be different. You're not as warm as Grace, but you don't want to be hurt; I can tell that. You'll do anything, Vicky, won't you, not to be hurt? And that's good. That'll make you the best! And you're such a skinny, pretty little thing ... I'm really looking forward to this! I hope you are, too."

He leaned in towards me. He sounded almost anxious.

"If you could just get yourself in the right frame of mind. If you –" He broke off. "Pardon me? You wanted to say something?"

"Why – didn't you –"

"Why didn't I – ?"

"Take – take her –"

"Take Grace? To the Bois? Is that what you're trying to say? It's a good question; I don't mind answering it. One reason was, there's been too much publicity. I never wanted that. I'm not one of those who craves attention. I just like to get on with things quite quietly in my own way. But they have to go and splash it all over the front pages, go frightening people off. To be honest, I didn't think she'd come with me. Not only that, it was time for a change. I don't believe one should become obsessive about these things. You need to vary the scenario every now and again otherwise there's a danger you grow stale. That's why –"

He shunted, his pale eyes behind the spectacles glinting mischievously.

"When you called me tonight I thought, Tracey, I thought, *carpe diem*. Do you know what that means? No? You obviously didn't have a classical education. It means, seize the day. Take the opportunity. I never thought you and I would get to be intimate, Vicky, what with that French faggot always hanging around. I guess he has to be a faggot. But I'm not prejudiced. I liked his dancing. That was nice. That put me in a good mood."

He shunted again, his mouth curving into a reminiscent grin.

"I had fun that night. They don't know about it yet. They'll discover! That was the last of my sylvan adventures – oh, I beg your pardon! I was forgetting. You don't have a classical education. That was my last excursion into the Bois. It's just as well; it doesn't do to glut. From now on –" he nodded, seriously – "from now on, it's an indoor game. They'll have to change that terrible nickname, won't they? How about…"

He flung back his head, squinting up at the light.

"How about, Butcher of the Boudoir? That has a ring, don't you think? And you can be his first celebrant. We won't count Grace; she was in the transition period. The Butcher of the Boudoir is born tonight!"

He swung me away from the wall. Involuntarily, I screamed. Screamed and screamed and went on screaming, my fear bouncing off the walls, filling the room with waves of terror. His hand clamped itself over my mouth.

"Vicky, I told you not to do that! I told you, I told you! I can't take it! Now I shall have to hurt you. I didn't want this! I wanted it to be a nice experience – for both of us! You stupid, stupid –" He was almost weeping. "*Stupid!* Gone and ruined everything! I warned you! I told you! I can't take the noise! I c—"

He stopped. The front door had suddenly crashed open and Jean-Guy was in the room.

"What the –"

"*JEAN-GUY!*" I screamed it at the top of my voice. "Jean-Guy, be careful!"

The next few seconds were a blur. I remember falling, and hitting my head against something. I remember seeing the sudden flash of a knife and bodies heaving to and fro. I remember hearing thuds and bangs and the overturning of furniture. I remember – I think – the angry slamming of a door somewhere below and footsteps pounding on the stairs. I remember seeing Jean-Guy do a high kick that a can-can dancer would not have been ashamed of, and hearing the clatter of steel on the parquet floor. I remember thinking, that will teach him to call Jean-Guy a French faggot...

And then I must finally have passed out, for I remember no more.

10

It was Sunday morning; late on Sunday morning. Eleven o'clock, to be exact. We could afford to be late. Sunday was our free day – no classes, no rehearsals, no performance.

We were sitting on the pavement in the sunshine, outside the café Fleury, me, Jean-Guy and Fernando. Fernando was looking glum, and frowning into his coffee cup; Jean-Guy and I were holding hands beneath the table. The reason Fernando was looking glum was that we still hadn't heard anything from Claire. The reason Jean-Guy and I were holding hands – but that can keep! I'll go into that later. (Maybe.)

It was Claire, at the moment, who was on our minds. Not that we any longer had fears for her safety – well, Jean-Guy and I didn't. Under pressure from the police Mme Dastugue had finally opened up and admitted that Claire had poured out the whole story of her broken engagement with Fernando. (Another surprise! My reticent twin baring her soul to a dour French concierge. Mme Dastugue was obviously more *sympathique* than one gave her credit for.) Claire had decamped, she said, "for reasons of the emotions", as Jean-Guy later translated it for my benefit, but where she had decamped *to* was another matter. That was something she had not divulged, or possibly Mme Dastugue had not troubled herself to ask.

"*Elle reviendra.*"

"Exactly what I've said all along," said Jean-Guy.

"Meaning what?"

"Meaning she'll come back when she's good and ready."

I sighed. "I still don't know what I'm going to tell Mum."

I was going to have to ring her tonight, before she started one of her panics. It would certainly panic her to learn that one of us had gone missing "for reasons of the emotions". Knowing Mum, she would catch the first flight over. I could just see her and Fernando tearing their hair out together.

"Just think," urged Jean-Guy, trying, I suppose, to be of comfort, "if she *hadn't* gone off she might even now be – well! One dreads to think."

"That's right," I said, eager to reinforce the message. "She had a date with Tracey that very same Sunday."

Poor Fernando! Far from solacing him our efforts seemed only to cause even greater anguish, for he groaned and said that if it hadn't been for him and his boorish insistence on "our children being brought up as Catholics", Claire would never had had anything to do with Tracey in the first place.

"It didn't sound to me as if you were particularly boorish." Jean-Guy reached out with his free hand for his cup of coffee. "If you're going to be conventional enough to do something like getting married, then presumably you have to discuss how you're going to handle the results of that marriage."

Fernando lifted his head, scowling. He directed his piercing gaze at me. (There were moments even now when he sent shivers down my spine.)

"You didn't believe me," he said. "Did you? When I said we were engaged ... you didn't believe me!"

I squirmed. "It just seemed so unlike Claire," I pleaded.

"Not at all," said Jean-Guy. "I disagree. Claire is a very proper-minded young woman – unlike some I could mention." His hand, under the table, squeezed mine. "She's not going to go tumbling into bed without having everything signed, sealed and delivered and a ring on her finger. It may surprise you to learn —" he addressed himself sternly to me — "there are still people in this world who believe in the old values."

I giggled, and then stopped. It might be a giggling matter to me and Jean-Guy, but it wasn't to Fernando. He was glowering at me across the table, heavy lids half lowered over deep-set eyes. If looks could scorch, I'd have singed at the edges. Imagine Claire, strait-laced, ever-so-English Claire, having a Latin lover! Or at least — I corrected myself — a Latin *would-be* lover. It was true, as Jean-Guy said, that my twin is very proper-minded. I suppose one of us has to be.

"I hope," said Fernando — and by now I'd have been nothing but a pile of smouldering ashes — "you do not imply I would ever ask your sister to do something that was not right."

It was funny, but I knew then that everything he'd told us was the exact truth. For the first time I really believed, emotionally, that my twin had become engaged to this man. All the same, I couldn't help retorting that he'd apparently had no compunction about asking Grace Arnold to do "something that was not quite right" — with truly devastating consequences.

Perhaps I shouldn't have said it; perhaps in the circumstances it wasn't fair. But moral pomposity really gets me.

Fernando's face, which is dark to begin with,

turned several shades darker. He said stiffly that "That was different."

"Why? Because you didn't want to marry her?"

"Grace was a different sort of girl."

Yes, and she had paid the price. Hadn't she just. I fell silent. I couldn't help reflecting that if I had never told Tracey about her that night, Grace would still be alive. I was the one who'd put the idea of Grace into his head. If I hadn't, if he'd suggested instead that I meet him for a cup of coffee, would I have been stupid enough to do so? I didn't think that I would, but you never know just how foolish you can be until the moment comes.

"Anyway," I said, trying feebly to make amends, "Jean-Guy believed you."

"Well, at least I didn't *not* believe him," said Jean-Guy. "At least I preserved an open mind. With the other guy – I don't know. There was just something about his story which didn't hang together. Something which kept prodding at me, only I couldn't quite manage to put my thumb on it."

Later, much later, I found the courage to confess to him that I, too, had had something which had prodded at me – something which I couldn't quite manage to put my thumb on. How, I asked him, had he been so certain it wasn't Claire he had seen on that mortuary slab?

"*Did* you know about her birthmark?"

He said that he had always known about it. He

reminded me that one summer when we were tiny, I mean really tiny, about ten months old and as like as two peas in a pod, we'd gone to stay with Auntie Vi while Mum was in hospital. Jean-Guy apparently – a sobering thought! – had helped Auntie Vi to bath us and change our nappies. He was very well acquainted with Claire's birthmark...

"The only way anyone could tell you apart!"

So simple – and it had never even occurred to me. Any more than it had occurred to me that there was something about Tracey which didn't hang together. Jean-Guy admitted that it hadn't struck him immediately. It wasn't until after Grace had been found murdered that he had started asking himself questions. The first question he had asked was how come Tracey had been immediately familiar with the rue des Soeurs when Jean-Guy, who knew Paris like the back of his hand, had never even heard of it?

The answer, of course, was that Tracey's apartment block was in the same *quartier*, only five minutes away. Not that that in itself had seemed to have very much significance. Only when he read in the papers the next day that the language school which both Grace and Claire had attended was also in the same *quartier*, and also only five minutes away, had he begun to wonder...

Tracey knew Claire; might he not also have known Grace?

Fernando, of course, by his own admission, knew both of them; and Fernando, also by his own admission, had been intimate with Grace. By rights, therefore, Fernando should have been the prime suspect.

But...

Fernando leaned forward, intently.

"It suddenly hit me," said Jean-Guy. "Right between the eyes ... when I got back from the party and they gave me your message, I suddenly knew what it was that had been bothering me. That day when you bumped into him, coming out of the flat –"

How had Tracey known that I was me and not Claire?

Fernando hadn't known that I was me. Fernando had grabbed me, thinking I was my twin.

"I wouldn't now," said Fernando, giving me a dirty look. I definitely wasn't his favourite person.

"You wouldn't now," agreed Jean-Guy, "because you've had a chance to sort out the differences."

"Yes," said Fernando, "I have!"

"But you hadn't then – and neither had the Yank. So how was he so sure?"

"The note!" I said. It was all coming clear. "It must have been him who broke in that night –"

"And read the note –"

"Which you always said you'd left lying on the table."

"Yes, and you as good as accused me of doing away with it!"

"I didn't, it was just that I couldn't think where it had gone. He must have taken it with him."

"So what did it say," said Fernando, "this note?"

I was surprised. "Didn't we ever tell you?" I turned to Jean-Guy. "We never told him!"

Jean-Guy did another of his shrugs.

"It just said –" I concentrated, trying to remember. "Sorry not here to meet you, had to go off, see you soon – oh, and it started 'Dear Identikit'. That's what we call each other," I said.

"So when the Yank saw you coming out of the flat next day he knew at once who you were – Vicky and not Claire. He just made the mistake of being too clever. Or not quite clever enough. If he'd had the wit to call you Claire, I'd never have been suspicious."

It had been that one little slip, perpetually nagging at him, at the back of his mind, which had made Jean-Guy so determined never to let me be on my own with Tracey.

"And to think I imagined it was because you might be jealous," I sighed. Of course I hadn't really imagined anything of the kind, but it was fun to tease. I could do that now.

Jean-Guy pressed my hand underneath the table. Our relationship had been ... slightly different since that night when Jean-Guy had come charging in like the Seventh Cavalry. We had had to go off to the police station, of course, and answer loads of questions, but what had been left of the night we had spent together, in the flat. And this time I hadn't woken up with arthritis of the spine.

"So tell us," I said, feeling that maybe we weren't paying enough attention to my sister's poor brooding boyfriend, "what made you believe Fernando's story? About him and Claire being engaged?"

I still maintained that on the face of it it was the very last thing you would expect. Fernando was far too exotic and sultry for my basic, down-to-earth twin.

"What she is trying to say," explained Fernando, "is why did you believe the sinister foreign chap? All foreign chaps are liars, yes?"

"Well, but Jean-Guy is a foreign chap, too," I said.

"Not in this country." Fernando swivelled his burning black eyes upon me and scorched me for the second time. "This is France, yes? And he is French, no?"

Jean-Guy gave a little smirk.

"All right," I said. "So why *did* you believe the sinister foreign chap?" Especially, I might have added, when he actually had lied about going to Brazil.

Jean-Guy said he didn't really know — "A gut feeling, I guess." Or maybe, he added, it was the way Fernando had leapt at me, shouting "Claire!" Maybe subconsciously, even then, he had been comparing Fernando's reaction to Tracey's.

Fernando sunk his head into his hands. He groaned. "I was so sure that you were her!"

"Oh, now, look," I said, bracingly, "she's bound to turn up. Let's run over all the possibilities just one more time."

I didn't want to run over all the possibilities; I wanted Fernando to finish his coffee and go on his way so that Jean-Guy and I could be alone together. But he was plainly distraught and having practically, in my own mind, labelled him a maniac if not an actual murderer, I felt the least I could do to make amends was show a little sympathy.

"We know she hasn't gone home, or Mum would have told me."

There was Granny Masters, but she lived in Malta; Claire was hardly very likely to have gone there. Apart from anything else, where would she have got the money? Then there were a couple of aunties, but one was in America and the other in the far flung north of Scotland, and in any case we hadn't seen either of them since we were about five years old. The probability still seemed to be that she had gone off with someone from the language school, but I scarcely liked to suggest it yet again. I kept suggesting it, and Fernando kept saying that she wasn't friendly with anyone at the language school, "not enough to go away with." It was beginning to have an air of desperation, as if it were the only thing I could think of – which in fact it was. I rummaged frantically through my brain, trying to come up with something else.

"You don't suppose," I cried, on a sudden note of inspiration, "that she saw one of those ads saying *Young people under twenty-five* and went rushing off to climb Mount Everest or – or go riding in the Pyrenees or –" my voice faltered – "or whatever it is they do," I finished lamely.

There was a silence.

"You mean an activity holiday," said Jean-Guy.

"Yes!" I seized on it, brightly. "An activity holiday!"

There was another silence.

"Well, why not?" I said.

"It doesn't sound much like Claire."

He'd got a nerve! I'd been saying all along that *none* of this sounded like Claire. Jean-Guy was the one who kept telling me that Paris did strange things to people.

I pointed this out to him and he said he meant emotionally. It did strange things to people emotionally. He said if I could picture my twin climbing Mount Everest or riding a horse in the Pyrenees in the company of two-dozen assorted under-twenty-fives, then I had a far more vivid imagination than he had ever given me credit for.

"All right!" I snapped. "So you come up with a suggestion! Where do you think she is?"

Jean-Guy was about to go into yet another of his shrugging routines – his shoulders, in fact, had got about half-way to his ears – when he suddenly stopped and his jaw fell open. It's the first and only time I've ever known him look less than godlike. I turned my head to see what he was staring at, and my jaw also fell open. There, swinging towards us on the opposite side of the street, wearing T-shirt and jeans and a pair of rather snazzy sunglasses, a canvas bag casually slung over her shoulder, was my identical twin. If I hadn't been sitting in the sunshine drinking coffee, with my hand firmly tucked into Jean-Guy's, I might almost have thought that it was me.

"Claire!"

Fernando sprang to his feet, rocking the table as he did so. I don't think, until that point, that Claire had seen us. At the sound of Fernando's voice she came to a halt. Her head jerked round. Slowly she raised a hand and pushed her sunglasses up.

For just a second they stood frozen, the pair of them, like bits of statuary; then Fernando rushed forward and Claire took a dive into the traffic and the next thing I know they're clasped in each other's arms in the middle of the pavement, standing there oblivious amongst all the Sunday-morning baguette-carriers on their way home from mass.

Jean-Guy and I just sat and gaped. I had the oddest sensation, just for a moment, that I had become Claire and she had become me. I thought, Jean-Guy is right: Paris does do strange things to people. Very strange indeed!

Afterwards, when the big hug was over, we all four sat round the table, only this time we ordered wine and while two of us still held hands discreetly *underneath* the table, two of us held hands quite openly on *top* of the table, and even broke off every now and again to exchange distinctly passionate kisses. Quite embarrassing, really, when it's your own twin sister. Not a sight you particularly want to sit and look at, though naturally I was happy for her and relieved to have her back. It meant I didn't have to worry any more about what I was going to say when I rang Mum that night.

"But where have you *been*?" I demanded.

"Have you been horse riding in the Pyrenees?" said Jean-Guy. "Or climbing up Mount Everest with a party of under-twenty-fives?"

"No." Claire sounded mystified. "Why should I be doing that?"

"Well, it seemed a better alternative than doing something silly to yourself, which is what your dearly beloved thought."

Claire blushed; so did Fernando. They exchanged another of their passionate kisses. Jean-Guy looked at me and rolled his eyes. Then he leaned towards me and whispered just two words, "*Plus tard*," which I think means "Later on." Then I blushed, too, but not Jean-Guy. He just grinned.

"So, come on!" I turned back to Claire. "Give! Spill the beans! What have you been up to?"

It was then, suitably shamefaced, she told us: she had run off to the South of France to be with Auntie Vi. (Auntie Vi! The one person we had never thought of.) She confessed she had been in a state after breaking off her engagement to Fernando.

"I know it sounds silly –" She gazed beseechingly into Fernando's eyes. Under the table, Jean-Guy's foot pressed against mine. "I know it sounds silly, but I just had to get away!"

She had felt the need to sort herself out and reckoned Auntie Vi was the person to help her do it, which apparently she had been. (Auntie Vi was always one for talking sound good sense.) It had never occurred to Claire that anyone might be worried about her, though she had felt bad about leaving the flat in such a mess.

"It was all so unlike you," I grumbled. "We were having these terrible visions –" And then I stopped, because I realized that Claire had no idea of the appalling events that had taken place in her absence. "We thought that somebody might have frightened you," I muttered.

"Frightened me?" Claire's eyes opened wide, very big and blue like a china doll's. (Horrid to think

that that's what mine look like. I made a mental note
there and then never to bat them at people.) "What
made you think that?"

There was a pause.

"This American —" said Fernando.

"He's Canadian, actually," I said. I thought it was
about time to set the record straight. Not that it
really made any difference.

Fernando glared at me. "This *Canadian*," he said.

Claire was looking from one to the other of us,
puzzled.

"Tracey?" I said.

"Oh! Tracey." Her cheeks coloured up. "Has he
been pestering you? He came and sat with me one
day when I was having a coffee, after —" she dipped
her head — "after we had that idiotic row. He talked
me into going to the cinema with him. I don't know
why I said yes. I suppose — oh, I don't know! I
suppose —"

"I understand," said Fernando.

"He got to be a real nuisance. He kept ringing me
up and calling round and begging me to go out with
him. I had to keep making excuses."

"Just as well you did," I said.

"Why?" Her eyes flickered across the table. "Has
— something happened?"

Fernando and I were both too cowardly to tell
her: we left it to Jean-Guy. He broke the news as
well as he could, avoiding all mention of Grace.

150

That, he obviously thought, would be better coming from Fernando when they were alone together.

"Vicky, that is so awful!" Claire's face was drained of colour – not that either of us has much to begin with. We have that kind of milky skin that so often goes with red hair. "You might have been killed and then I would never have forgiven myself!"

"Well, I wasn't," I said, stoutly. "But I do think," I added, "that you ought to apologize for all the trouble you've caused."

In a meek voice, quite unlike her normal confident tones, Claire said: "I'm sorry. I apologize."

I blinked. Whatever was the world coming to?

When I rang Mum that night we had this zany conversation about next door's ground ivy which was creeping under the fence and into Mum's flower-bed and choking all her bedding plants. At the end she said, "And you and Claire ... are you getting on all right?"

"Fine," I said.

"That's nice! I always said you'd start to rub along better as you grew older. How are you enjoying Paris? Anything exciting happening?"

"Not really," I said. "Just the same old routine ... class, rehearsal, performance. Nothing out of the ordinary."

"And Jean-Guy's keeping an eye on you?"

"Yes, yes," I said.

"He's a good boy; I knew I could rely on him. I never worry when he's there. And Claire, of course; she's always had an old head on her shoulders. You're the scatty one."

"That's right," I said.

I didn't tell her about Paris making people do strange things. Making them act out of character. Even Jean-Guy, these past couple of days ... except maybe in his case it wasn't so out of character after all. One thing I had learnt since coming to Paris, you can't necessarily believe all that you're told.

Especially in a ballet company.

•PATSY KELLY•
INVESTIGATES

When Patsy starts work at her uncle's
detective agency, her instructions are very
clear. Do the filing. Answer the phone.
Make the tea. *Don't* get involved in any
of the cases.

But somehow Patsy can't help
getting involved...

And it's not just the cases she has to worry
about. There's Billy, too. Will she ever work
out what she *really* feels about him...?

•PATSY KELLY•
INVESTIGATES

Anne Cassidy

Look out for:

A Family Affair
End of the Line

Dare you unlock...

THE SECRET DIARIES

Dear Diary...

When Joanna starts at her new school, she suddenly has a lot to write about in her diary. For one thing, she's fallen madly in love...

I'm not sure I want to write this down, Diary...

But then she finds her love leads her to write about other things. Betrayal and danger. Maybe even murder...

At least I know my secret will be safe with you. Though you wouldn't think safety was a big concern of mine. Not after I got involved in such terrible things...

Discover Joanna's shocking secrets in *The Secret Diaries* by Janice Harrell:

I Temptation
II Betrayal
III Escape

All the thrills of a busy Emergency Room,
from the ever-popular Caroline B. Cooney.

EMERGENCY ROOM

**CITY HOSPITAL.
EMERGENCY ROOM. And
the evening has only just
begun...**

**6.00 p.m. Volunteers Diana
and Seth arrive – eager to
help save lives...**

**6.38 p.m. Emergency – gun
shot wound – victim of a
deadly drug battle...**

**6.55 p.m. Suspected cardiac
in Bed 8. Another routine
heart attack? Not for
Diana...**

**7.16 p.m. All systems go –
Alec, sixteen, clings to life by
a thread.**

**This is the Emergency Room.
Precious seconds are ticking
away, and Diana and Seth
hold the balance between life
and death...**

Point Horror

Are you hooked on horror? Are you thrilled by fear? Then these are the books for you! A powerful series of horror fiction designed to keep you quaking in your shoes.